VERMIN

Adrienne Silcock

FLAMBARD

First published in England in 2000 by Flambard
Stable Cottage, East Fourstones, Hexham NE47 5DX

Typeset by Harry Novak
Cover design by Gainford Design Associates
Printed by Cromwell Press, Trowbridge, Wiltshire

A CIP catalogue record for this book
is available from the British Library

ISBN 1 873226 41 1

Flambard wishes to thank Northern Arts for its financial support.

CONTENTS

VERMIN

SIS

Somebody once suggested to me that my sister Gloria had turned out like that because she was angry. But I don't think so. Anger is a different thing altogether, isn't it? She's disturbed, and that's all there is to it.

GLORIA

When you asks what I'm doin here an I says, 'fuckin rubbish', I ain't bein rude, nor disrespectful. The truth is, that's just how it began... with a pile of stinkin rubbish dumped in a skip... an if it hadn't bin for that rubbish, I wouldn't be where I am now, though I can't say I might not of landed up here some time through some other set of circumstances, if you gets what I mean. After all, that's life, en it?

Some geezer's havin a clear-out, yer see. Each day the skip in the yard grows deeper with discarded goodies, an each day I loiters, wonderin if this time I might dare have a rummage. I knows there's some good stuff in there; I can see things pokin out from mongst the old plaster board an tiles an the bags of stinkin nappies. An old beige armchair, one of those wingback ones. A piece of old carpet, a flowery pattern, in purples, what would do for the kitchen. For now at any rate. Till me ship comes in... ha ha, that's a joke – 'till me ship comes in'! As if someone like me could afford a ship! Me, I couldn't raise a mortgage on a fuckin row-boat.

It's a big yella skip with black writin on the side. S.J. an sommat. I can't read it, can't make it out. Never did get on top of that one, yer see.

'Clear off,' a bloke shouts, 'don't want none of your sort round here.'

Blast, I thinks.

I'd chosen a day when it's pissin it down, deliberate like. This'll be a good day to have a rummage, I says to meself as I prises meself outta bed that mornin. Me hair's drippin, water's dribblin down me neck. Skoodlin, I likes to call it. I likes makin up words an skoodlin is just what it feels like, the water runnin down me neck, soakin into me old wool sweater, skoodlin down into it. Fuckin freezin an all. Comin down in sheets, the rain is, like me own private curtains. No-one'll see, an no-one'll care, I thinks, no-one'll be out nosin in this.

I've just rolled up me sleeves. I've had a good look in first, like, could see this jacket that I thinks would do for Jim even if it hangs like a dog's bollocks on me. I used to see him sometimes, yer see. Jim, I mean. Around, yer know. In the park. Down the benefit. In the street. We sometimes talked. Other times we passed each other like strangers. When neither of us had nothin worth sayin. Or he was high. Way out of it. Or I was low. So fuckin low me chin was practically draggin along the pavement.

Anyway, I'm just in the middle of landin this jacket, when he starts shoutin. The bloke, I mean, not Jim. He shouts, 'Oy, you!' He's standin in his doorway on the other side of the yard in his shirt sleeves, great hairy arms folded, muscles bulgin, lumpy as sacks of taters. An she's standin behind him all fuckin dainty and pink in her angora jumper and a gold chain round her neck. An there's a brat standin by her legs, tuggin at her black ski-pants, its gob caked with chocolate or some such. Yeah, the whole bleedin family, like family show time. Shall I take a bow, I thinks to meself.

'Clear off,' he shouts. I don't say nothin. Just turns an walks away, cursin under me breath. It's only their fuckin rubbish, I thinks. They've thrown it out. They doesn't want it. But they doesn't want me to have it neither. Not even one fuckin jacket. Still, I promises meself I'll go back. I would of gone back in the dark if I'd had a torch. Maybe I could of lit a match or two. But I thinks, naa, daylight's the job. Then I can really have a good rummage.

SIS

She always was a bit of a collector of things, a hoarder. Mum used to call her the magpie, because she'd snaffle anything she could lay her thieving hands on into her bedroom, bits and pieces of Mum's make-up, mine as I got older, pencils, pens, the little silver mustard spoon that had been our Nan's, aluminium foil pie cases, in fact anything shiny whatsoever. And if anyone had lost something you could bet your bottom dollar it'd be somewhere in Gloria's room.

GLORIA

The skip's been there five, maybe six days. It's more than full, it's overflowin. There's old pictures, magazines, a mattress, yellowin nylon under-slips, a dressin gown. The jacket's long since buried. But I doesn't mind. There's other things. An aluminium saucepan, a couple of mugs. Not bad, only one or two small chips in them by the looks of it. An old hoover, a pale cream blanket with brown stains on it. Some floorboards, mealy with woodworm. But there's a lot of things there I thinks could be useful to me. I stands by the skip. It's like a large buttercup, all bright yella, an inside, the goodies. Like nectar to the bee. Climb inside, it's sayin. Pollinate. Yeah, I could fuckin pollinate a few of those fuckin things into me front room. Cept I've lost me nerve a bit. Since he came out an hollered at me.

Wasn't used to it, yer see. People hollerin at me. Not then. I'd got away from all that when I left home. Could say I'd opted for the quiet life. I didn't have much to do with nobody. Part from Jim sometimes, that is. Not that I has much to do with nobody in here neither. They hollers in here sometimes, an I still doesn't like it. Funny, en it, that I still can't stand it after all these years?

Anyhow, out there, people usually does their best to avoid me, crossin the street, steppin down from the pavement while they gets past, turnin their heads, pretendin to have their eye on sommat in a shop window, suddenly havin sommat rivetin to say to their friends. They can't stand to look you direct in the eye, yer see. Not that I really wants that. Quite frankly it's the last fuckin thing I wants. There's them down the benefit, been trained, yer know. Looks at you straight, they does, eyebrows like fuckin crescent moons above their eyes, trying to look open-minded, honest. Honest, my arse. Sits there, they does, pretendin to listen to what you're tryin to say, all the while thinkin about what they're goin to nosh for lunch, where they're goin to go in the evenin. What about nippin into Marks's for one of those chicken kievs, one said to her pal once. Right in front of me, it was. We could pick up a bottle of Chablis, oh and some garlic bread with herbs. Good idea, says the other, then we'll go down to Charley's for a couple. It's all right for the haves, I says. Not to their faces, like. I stands there all meek an quiet an grateful-lookin like yer meant to, but all the while I'm thinkin, yeah, it's all right for the haves. What about the fuckin have-nots?

What's that? I'm sounding bitter? Too bloody right I am. See, they doesn't know what it's like. They says, oh, but we can't afford this an we can't afford that an it's all right for so an so, an makes jokes about how the other half does it an winnin the lottery an stuff, but they just doesn't know how it feels to be standin outside somebody else's skip in the pissin bloody rain, water skoodlin down your neck, ooglin somebody else's old jacket. Not that there'll be much bloody wrong with that jacket. That's just the point. There ain't nothin wrong with it. It's just that somebody don't want it because it ain't the fashion, or it's the wrong colour or some such item. An I could of given it to Jim, to keep him warm. Bloody consumer society, that's what they calls it, yer know. Consumer society. Gobble bloody gobble.

I wants to reach in an take those mugs for starters. I looks around. No-one's about. The house where the bloke an his missus lives is all curtained up. I can hear a kid cryin inside. That touches me, it does. Never could abide kids cryin. But everywhere else is quiet. An autumn leaf scratches like a rat across the yard. I reaches in an nabs the mugs, darts off back round the corner. I'll go again in a minute, I says to meself. Just… blast, I realises that I haven't got a fuckin bag to put them in. If Jim was there he would of said this ain't Marks an fuckin Spencer's now yer know. Next thing you'll be wantin is a fuckin till receipt. I shoves the mugs into the pockets of me overcoat. Nice big pockets, an the holes ain't big enough for the mugs to slip through. Now, I asks meself, what shall I have next?

I thinks that the coast is clear an I nips back round the corner.

I quite fancies the dressin gown. I'll have that. It'll need a good
wash, I'll have to take it down the laundromat, but it's in good
nick. I'm just tryin to pull it out when I hears this shout from
behind me. It's the same fuckin voice as before.

'Oy you,' it says, 'told you to clear off th'other day, dint I?'

I lets go of the dressin gown an turns to look at him. It takes
all me courage but I stares into his scowlin face. I sees him
wince a bit, embarrassed like.

'Bloody hell,' he says, 'thought you was a bloke.'

Look, Mister, I wants to say, what's the harm, I'm only
wantin a few things to keep Ol' Glory goin over the winter,
you're chuckin em out, en't yer, an it'll save me a few coppers –
I won't make a mess, promise. But it doesn't come out like
that.

'Mean fuckin cunt,' I says.

For a minute I thinks he's goin to take a swing at me, his
lips scrunch up like he's holdin all his anger in. But I doesn't
hang around to see if me number's come up. I'm off. Hops it.
Skedaddles across the yard fast as me pegs'll carry me.

'If I see you again round here,' he says, 'I'll call the fuckin
police.'

I doesn't know why but at that moment something catches me
eye an I pauses a second to glance up at the top window of his
house. The little kid what I saw the other day is standin with his
nose pressed against the pane. Next to him is an older boy, his
brother, I guess, starin out at me an all. An suddenly I realises
that they've bin kneelin at that window for a while without me
realisin. Watchin me.

'Scram!' yells the bloke, seein me pause.

I doesn't wait for another invitation. Fuck knows, I'd had
enough excitement for one mornin. In any case the wind's got
up an I've a feelin I can smell rain an I doesn't fancy another
soakin like the time before, so I decides not to go nowhere else
but to head for home. Cross the park. No sign of Jim, but I curses
about the jacket. Would of just suited him an all, I says to meself.

Along to our block. The lift's bust again, fuckin vandals, so I goes up the stairs. Stinks of piss, they does. Mind you so does the lift these days. An the walls are daubed with SHARON LOVES WAYNE and FUCK OFF WANKERS. Terrible language youngsters today. I lets meself in, an somehow comin to that dim bare room gives me a downer, right low I feels. All that trampin around, me corns achin, me sciatica fuckin me legs up, an all I've got is a couple of soddin mugs to show for it, not even the bleedin dressin gown. I retrieves the mugs from me pockets, places em on the table in the kitchen. They're OK. Can't see em usin them in the Ritz, like, on account of the chips. Ha, ha, that's a fuckin laugh, en it, they doesn't serve chips in the Ritz! Get it?

Pale blue, those mugs. Plain, like. Quite a pretty colour. But all of a sudden I feels a surge of rage an picks one up an smashes it against the fuckin wall. Crash it goes. Bits of blue everywhere. Cos, yer see, it got to me. Me. There. Stuck in that fuckin state. Couldn't afford to go out an buy a mug without a fuckin chip in it. Got me fuckin angry. There, in that bloody flat with the damp patch in the corner what the council have still gotta come an fix. Not exactly cosy, was it?

I sits on the floor for a while, asks meself what's the use in gettin upset? I should spend some of me benefit on paint and cheer the place up, make it light and airy, brilliant white or sommat. But then I tells meself that it would fust up again unless they fixes it first, which they won't. An when do *I* have cash left for paint an such after me livin expenses, as it were?

Sometimes I didn't mind it, like. But that day it must've just about pierced me fuckin skin. Sittin there on me own. The walls cavin in on me, dark and dreary.

Then, just as sudden like, I cheers up. Cos I has an idea. Maybe if I was to pull back the net (the only curtain I had) an give the windows a wipe it would let some more light in. Somehow that day I felt like I was drownin in darkness, strugglin to come up for a breath of light.

So, I gets up, opens the frenchie an stands out on the balcony for a minute starin out over the town. The sky's the colour of cement, looks like the whole fuckin lot is goin to churn up an plop down on us like out of a gigantic concrete mixer. I goes back inside an lights a fag. First one of the day. Good, en't I? Two or three a day and that's me limit. For the good of me health. An me pocket of course.

Then I gets a bucket an an old pair of drawers an fills the bucket with water. There ain't no hot. I didn't used to switch the mersion on much. Kept a check on the old electric, like. Just like I didn't use the lights much neither. Little as poss any rate. Sometimes they used to cut me off, an I'd end up with all these nosy buggers round, talkin bout budgets an fuckin direct payment plans an stuff. Bloody hell, a dame can do without that sorta crap, can't she.

Anyhow, I washes down the windows. Wipes. Rinses an squeezes out the cloth. Wipes again. Works up a good rhythm. Wants that jacket, wants it bad, wants that jacket, wants it bad, I croons to meself. Gets it done that way. An even though the water's fuckin freezin it actually seems to warm me up. The exercise, yer see. In fact I ain't realised how cold it is until I begins to get warm.

That's better, I says to meself when I've finished and goes an leaves the bucket by the sink. An I'm feelin cheered up. So much so that I thinks I owes meself a little celebration. Course when I inspects all the bottles on the kitchen table I can't find one with a drop in. Better go out for some, I thinks to meself, can't have Ol' Glory dyin of thirst. So off I goes. Back down the stairs, passes them kids again. Them I've seen everyday that week. Should of bin at school of course, but their ma's can't control em, yer know. Most of em ain't even got a dad. Not like in my day of course, when most of us had em an couldn't wait to leave home to be shot of em. Better off without em is what I says.

SIS

I remember as a child she used to fly into the most awful rages, ranting and raging something terrible. Frightened the wits out of me, she did, even though I was nearly five years older than her. I'd lock myself in the bathroom, or go out somewhere, anything to get away from her when she was like that. Mum used to turn the music on the radio up really loud to try to drown her out, but that usually brought the neighbours round complaining. She did get wild though. Even Dad would leave her alone when she was like that. Maybe that was why she did it, so as he *would* leave her alone.

GLORIA

I've just come out of the offie an I'm toddlin along the street,
feelin pleased with meself cos the British sherry was on special
offer when I spies Jim comin along towards me. Jim, I says, how
yer doin. He grunts at me. Doesn't look in a very good mood.
But I wants to tell him about the jacket.

'You looks cold, Jim,' I says.

'Eh?' he says, an stops, though he was gonna walk straight
by.

His hair's grey and frizzed. Right down to his shoulders, it is.
His beard grows out patchy, hangs in bunches like dreadlocks.
Someone should take him in hand, give him a good old wash
an brush up, I thinks to meself.

'You cold, Jim?' I asks.

'Could be a bit.'

His words slur together in a deep rumble. There's those that'd
be hard pushed to make out what he's sayin, but I'm used to it,
an what I can't make out, I guesses.

'I've seen just the jacket for you,' I says.

'Where's that then,' he says, 'Harrods?'

'I might have a bit of a job getting hold of it like,' I says, 'but
it's a real nice colour, keep yer nice an warm too.'

'Hey,' he rumbles, 'don't go gettin up to no monkey business
on my be'alf. I ain't askin no favours.'

'Well, let's say if I gets it for you I gets it, an if I doesn't I
doesn't.'

'Hmph,' he says an trundles off towards the offie.

Just as he's going up the steps, he turns an waggles his arm
at me. There's a good-natured sparkle in his eye.

'Thanks, Glory.'

Well, I goes home an has a little drink, finds a bit of bread an a
Cup-a-Soup for me lunch, an has a little snooze on me bed.

When I wakes up the cement sky has turned into asphalt an the street lights are just comin on. I gets up, draws the net across the frenchie, thinks of turnin a light on, but thinks better of it, then decides I might go out, have another go at that jacket an such like, I ain't got nothin better to do. An I don't like that empty flat neither.

It's cold out. Wouldn't be surprised if it snowed though it's only November. I makes sure I buttons me coat right up, pulls me scarf round me neck. Good job I has me trousers on, couldn't be doin with no dress flappin round me legs, draughts freezin me fanny.

When I gets to the yard I notices there's a couple of kids snoggin just along from the skip. I stands in the shadows.

'What's that?' I hear the girl say in a nervous voice.

I doesn't move.

'Nothin,' the boy replies, 'now where were we?'

'I'm sure I heard sommat,' she's sayin.

'Rats,' he says. 'It'll be rats in the rubbish.'

'Bloody hell,' she says, 'I dunt like rats.'

'They ain't gonna come near ya,' he says. 'Now come here.'

An they starts up again.

I feels embarrassed like, thinks about slippin away again, comin back later. But then I thinks of the jacket, the dressing gown an that table lamp I saw too, an I stays right where I am, tryin to be quiet, thinkin maybe if I was to give up me two or three fags per day, the breath in me chest wouldn't rasp with such a bleedin racket. Still, them kids ain't takin no more notice. I stands there, listenin to the traffic out on the main road. Somewhere a child's cryin an all. I thinks it's comin from where that bloke an his missus lives, the ones what seems to know bout the skip. Yeh. Come to think of it, it's the same cryin what I heard the other day, an I hear that bloke's voice too. Shoutin. Unpleasant, like. Makes me shudder. Reminds me of what He was like (Him with a capital fuckin H, an I ain't talkin about our Lord neither) always shoutin an hollerin around the place, makin us kids feel like dirt, makin me Mum feel like dirt an all, I wouldn't wonder, though she never ever said nothin.

Suddenly their door swings open. It's the lovebirds turn to hide. They nestles into the corner while the lion comes roarin out of his den, slammin the door behind him, cuttin off the shaft of yella light that had shone out for a few moments onto the concrete yard, like cutting off a lump of butter. His footsteps go pat pat pat up the path, slappin against the wet surface. Yeh, it's started to piss it down again. Not snow yet, but drops cold as fuckin icicles. I looks up an catches sight of the lovebirds slinkin off towards town. I'm grinnin to meself now. The yard's all mine, at last.

I can't see too well. I've a matchbox in me pocket an I gets a match out to strike. I tries to light it, but it's pissin down that much the match is wet before it's got a chance. Fuck that for a laugh, I shoves the matchbox away before the darn thing gets soaked altogether. It's just then I feels a tug at the bottom of me coat. It gives me a hell of a fright an I'm just about to let out one of me more choice phrases when I sees it's that kid, what I saw before kneelin in the window, standin there right beside me.

'Blimey,' I says, 'you give me a fright!'

An then I thinks, bloody hell what if his Mum knows I'm here, maybe she's called the fuckin police.

'Yer Mum know I'm here?' I asks.

He shakes his head.

'No-one else?'

He shakes his head again.

'You're a bag lady, ent ya?' he says, sudden like. 'Me Mum says you're a bag lady.'

'Oh, I en't got no bag,' I says, suddenly rememberin I'd forgotten to shove one in me pocket before I come out. 'That's half the trouble,' I says. 'If I had a bag I could put the things I wanted into it, couldn't I?'

'What things did you want?' he asks.

'Well, there was a nice dressin gown in there, would of done me nicely. An that lamp,' I says, suddenly spotting it in the light from the house.

'That was me Nana's lamp.'

'Was it now,' I says. 'Very nice lamp it is too. Your Nana has good taste.'

'It's all me Nana's stuff. She's dead yer see. An we've moved in. An we're havin a big sort out.'

The kid's in his pyjamas.

'Shouldn't you be indoors?' I says. 'You'll be gettin cold and wet.'

'Naah,' he says, and starts trying to climb into the skip.

'Hey, stop that,' I says, 'you'll get all filthy.'

'Don't care,' he says.

'How d'you get out anyhow? I didn't see you comin out that door.'

'Didn't,' he says. 'I came round the back. Me Mum's gone up to have a bath an I slipped out that way so's she wouldn't hear. I was finkin about running away, then I saw you.'

'Runnin away?' I says. 'What'd you wanna do that for?'

Here's a funny little chap, I thinks to meself. Reminds me of me as a kid an all them times I wanted to run away.

He's stopped tryin to scramble up the side of the skip and is standin starin up at me. I couldn't really see, but there was a tear or two in his voice.

'I don't like me Dad,' he says.

There's a click of the front door across the yard, an outside light comes on, the buttery rays spreadin across the yard. I darts back into the darkness.

'Darren!' a woman's voice shouts. 'Darren, I know you're out there, our Darren. Come in, you naughty lad.'

It's a Northern voice. Low in tone. Not so posh as I'd imagined somehow, like I'd expected from her looks. Didn't quite fit in with the pink fluffy angora.

'Hey,' whispers Darren to me, 'come tomorra. Bring a bag, Bag Lady.'

'What time tomorra?' I whispers back.

'After school,' he says, 'before me Dad comes back from work.'

Another shout from across the yard.

'Eh, Darren, you talkin to someone out there?' goes the pink angora.

'Naa, Mum, I was playin a game.'

An he runs off into the house an his Mum shuts the door, takin the light with her.

It's so soddin dark in that corner by the skip that I knows I'm gonna have to give up pokin about in it unless I wants to get covered in shit. Anyhow, I'm gettin cold and I thinks I'll go home, see what I can rustle up to eat. I knows there's still some bread, an I thinks there's maybe a tin of spam in the cupboard. So I sets off, leavin them rats rustlin behind me.

SIS

Of course, he always gave her more trouble than he did me. I guess she was around more when he most wanted us to do it. It was the time when Mum had that fella on the side – oh, yes, I knew about that all right though I don't think she ever knew I knew, if you see what I mean. I was always off out with my boyfriend, that Sammy Smedley, bless him. I wonder whatever happened to him. But Glory, well, she was always in on account of her not having many friends. She'd come sobbing into me in the middle of the night sometimes, tell me what he'd done. But what could I do about it? If we'd objected or gone and complained to someone he would only have beaten the living daylights out of us, wouldn't he?

GLORIA

I dunno what made me do as that little kid told me. I mean, he could of gone in an said sommat to his Mum, and next day when I went his Dad could of bin waitin to beat the livin daylights out of me. But somehow I trusts him. An I wants to go back because I'm fool enough to think that somehow he needs me. This time I remembers to take a carrier. Stores em up, I do. Big bundle under the kitchen table, there is. Such a waste to chuck em out when they gives em to you free gratis at the corner store. Fact is, I never chucks nothin away what might come in useful some time. Could say I'm a conservationist, couldn't yer?

It's benefit day so I'm busy, an by the time I'm finished I sees it's sommat after three by the post office clock. I weren't too hot at tellin the time then, tho yer learns about things like that in here. And course I've bin fitted out with glasses what I didn't have then. Which helps. Tho sometimes I wishes I was like I was before, cos now I can tell the minutes on the clock they really seems to drag. Takes for ever to move from one hour to the next, it do. Specially when yer waitin for sommat. And yer always waitin for sommat in here, you are. Waitin for yer tea, waitin for yer visitor, waitin for fuckin *Coronation Street.* I'm sick of fuckin waitin. Clock-watchin, they calls it, don't they? Before, mostly anyhow, time used to drift by. Gentle as specks of dust in sunlight. There, but I'm forgettin the bad times, en't I? Yer always pushes them to the back, don't yer, eh?

Anyhow, that particular day, I looks at the clock, cos I've gotta meet Darren after school, en't I, so I trundles off outta the post office towards them mews houses an the skip. It's still light an I has to be careful who sees me. In fact just as I'm arrivin I sees Darren with his Mum, the pink angora, carryin his little brother. Darren's in school uniform. Somehow he looks too small to be wearin it, too small to be goin to school. The start of the big bad world, Lord bless 'im.

They doesn't see me. I hides in a doorway till they've gone, has a sly look in the skip from afar. Has meself a little drink from me flask. Next minute Darren's standin there, already changed into a track suit.

'Told me Mum I was coming out to play for a few minutes,' he says, smilin his cheeky little smile.

'She don't know I'm here, do she?' I asks, worried.

'Naa,' he grins.

So we sets to work straight away, digs out Darren's grandma's table lamp, which seems to be buried even deeper than ever. There's an alarm clock, which Darren says he don't know whether it works or not, but I takes it all the same. Never know, I thinks to meself, one of these days I might get clever with me hands an fix it if it don't work.

There's no sign of the jacket. I tells Darren about it. He says he knows already, he's seen me trying to pull it out the first time, when he was watching out the window. He says if he can get hold of it, he'll put it in a bag for the bag lady an save it for her. I says don't for heaven's sake go gettin into trouble on my account. He says he don't care. An I says, oh yeh, what was that about you wanting to run away? Then he looks all gloomy an says he hates his Dad. An rolls up his tracksuit bottom an shows me a dirty great bruise on his leg where he says his Dad kicked him. Grey-blue, it is. Grey-blue as the November darkness that's comin in. Gor blimey, I says, does he do that sort of thing often? Yeah, he says, almost matter of fact. An he hits me little brother, an me Mum. Does he now, I says. Anyhow you'd better get in now, lad, I says, thanks for your help. An he says he doesn't wanna go in. He never wants to go in, he's scared. An I says he has to for now. After all, I thinks to meself, where in the bleedin hell else would the poor little bugger go?

I says cheerio, an trundles off through the park with me bag of goodies. I don't see Jim, so I can't show him me treasure. Still never mind, I goes home and unpacks. Tomorra I'll see if I can buy a bulb for the lamp. I would of took the one outta the front room socket but it blew yesterday, so's I ain't got a light in the flat. I strikes a match an sees meself to bed, uses another one to light meself a fag an another to pour meself a little drink from the bottle besides the bed, though there ain't much left.

I lies in bed, but I can't stop meself thinkin bout little Darren. I doesn't usually think too much about other people. Yeh well, I thinks occasionally bout Jim, cos he was bout the only real friend I ever had, an even then he weren't much of a friend sometimes. An course I thinks bout me old Mum sometimes. But there's not many worth thinkin about, is there? But little Darren, well, already I was feelin that we was pals, even though he was scarcely seven an I was sommat over fifty.

But I'm worried. I had bin worryin about Jim's jacket, but then that don't seem important no longer. Stead, I'm worryin about Darren an the bruises on his legs, an the fresh ones that could be appearin right now on his pale little body. I wouldn't hurt him for the world. Funny, en it, me an a seven year old. But he was the only fucker I really felt I could talk to, where things came out of me head like I wanted them to, stead of bein all tongue-tied an end up swearin at people. Ain't so bad now. Talks to people sometimes. People like you, what's gonna listen, like. Though sometimes I gets narked and lets rip. Blimey, an then yer should see their faces!

Darren an me, though, we're good chums. An I was hopin to Christ his dad weren't givin him any more of a beatin that day. Cos, Christ, I knows how that feels.

SIS

After a while she took to being a bit of a wanderer. Used to go out at night (for walks, she said) when I was sitting doing my homework. Yes, because by then I'd decided that if I wanted to get anywhere in life I would have to buckle down and get my exams. And mostly he left me alone, thank Christ. But even if she did stay in, she never got anywhere with her school work. She used to complain about letters dancing about the page in front of her eyes. Perhaps that was the first sign. Of her madness, I mean. Oh, and headaches. Yes, she used to complain about headaches. Mum always told her to shut up and stop moaning. She didn't want anything to do with doctors, our Mum, though I think if it was me with our Sally – that was my little girl (though she's grown up now, you understand) – I would take her. After all, you never know what they can do for you nowadays, do you?

GLORIA

Next day I decides to go back. It's Saturday. We've made no arrangement, but I thinks well, he'll probably look out for me. But just as I'm comin out the park gates he passes me with a couple of his pals on the way in. They're carryin a football. He scarcely looks at me. An I thinks well the fuck that's what happens ain't it. People talks to you when they wants. Otherwise they don't wanna know. Anyhow, what would his friends say if he went speaking to a scruffy ol' gal like me dressed up in a gent's overcoat and a scarf on me head. So I turns round and goes and sits on a bench, watches the squirrels come out rummagin. Some says they're vermin, don't they, like rats an stuff, only with big bushy tails. But I likes to watch em. After all, they're only animals tryin to survive, ain't they?

So I sits an watches em scamperin about. Cos the day's mild for November, the sun still offerin a bit of heat. An I sits there, an I can see from afar Darren and his pals playing football, an me mind turns to wonderin about Jim, who I haven't now seen for almost a week.

Eventually I wanders home again. I thinks to meself, I'll buy a bottle of cider, have a liquid lunch, as it were. I'm feelin low. What else have I got to live for in this fuckin world?

I'm lyin on me bed, havin had sommat of a snooze, when there's a knock at the door. At least to begin with I don't think it's a knock, I thinks it's next door bashin about, but it comes again, louder. Fuckin hell police, I thinks. What've I done now? I looks through me spy hole, but I can't see no-one. There's a knock again, makes me nearly jump out of me bleedin skin, so I decides to open up and see what's goin on. I can't believe it when I sees little Darren standin there.

'What're you doin?' I says.

'Come to visit,' he says.

'How d'yer know where to find me?'

He told me he'd followed me back from the park earlier. He wanted to see where I lived, he said. Then he'd popped back to his pals to finish his game. Then thought he'd come visitin this afternoon. He had a proud little smile on his lips. A gleam in his eye.

'Thought you didn't see me,' I says, a bit sulky like.

He shrugs. 'Course I did,' he says.

'Yer a long way from home,' I says. 'Won't yer Mum be worried about yer?'

'She finks I'm in the park again,' he says. He wriggles, yanks at a trouser leg with one of his little hands, looks absent-mindedly about him.

'I s'pose you'd better come in,' I says, standin clear of the doorway, yet not wantin him to see the state of the place I has to call 'home'.

'You haven't got much, have you?' he says. 'Where's your telly?'

It's my turn to shrug. I'm feelin a bit irritable now.

'None of your flippin business,' I says.

But he doesn't say nothin, instead picks up a paper, one of those freebies they brings round, what I ain't bothered to pick up meself, picks it up from the floor behind the door, hands it to me. 'Yer paper,' he says.

'Oh, that ain't no good to me,' I laughs. 'Looks like a load of gobbledegook.'

'Why's that?' he says.

I'm needled now. I'm tremblin an I wanna call him a little shite an tell him to get out me house, but he's lookin up at me with those round curious eyes.

'I can't read, can I?' I accuse him. Half shoutin.

His bottom lip pushes out an begins to quiver. An straightway I feels sorry an goes over to him, offers an arm, tentative like.

'Look, kid, I'm sorry,' I says. 'It's not your fault, is it now?'

He's lookin thoughtful, his little brows pinched together. An then his face brightens.

'I'll tell you what,' he says, 'I'll bring me reading books here, an I can learn you what I learn at school, Bag Lady.'

'I wish you wouldn't call me that,' I laughs. 'It's Glory. Me name's Glory.'

Then I'm suddenly feelin low again.

'What's the matter, Glory?' Darren asks.

I sighs. 'I dunno, lad. Just wishes I had some sweets or sommat to give you.'

'Me Dad gives me sweets,' he says, 'tells me to go away and eat them. He doesn't want me, don't me Dad.'

I looks out the frenchie so he can't see the tear in me eye. See, me old man didn't want me neither. He didn't want me or Sis, cept when we was older. There was sommat he liked from us then. But I doesn't think about that. No. I never lets meself think about that.

The sky out the frenchie is blearin with dark blues an purples. To the east there's a golden strip of light linin the horizon makin the bricks an concrete, the leaves on the trees, all of them orange.

'You'd better be gettin home, lad,' I says.

'Don't wanna go,' he says.

'Look, lad,' I says, 'you'll only make things worse for yourself if you don't go.'

At last he agrees, then I has an idea an offers to walk back with him, see him safe.

We walks along in silence, like old buddies. When we're nearly there, he says, are you comin tomorra. Yes, lad, I says. I'll come for the jacket tomorra.

Course I can't sleep that night neither. I can't think if I'm feelin more sorry for little Darren or meself. See, we're in the same boat en't we, only time's set me free from that one. Well, sort of free. Cos you ain't really ever free when you've bin treated like that. Yer thoughts prison yer, don't they? Set railings round what yer does, handcuff yer to an existence what yer could do without.

In the same boat as Darren. Funny these sayins, en't they? 'In the same boat.' 'When me ship comes in.' 'Plain sailin.' Like life's a long sea voyage. Helluva lot of stormy fuckin weather.

Then sommat sets me off thinkin bout sweets an how Darren weren't really fussed about em, only sees em as sommat what's offered to get him out of the way. Funny, me thinkin I wanted to give him some to show what I think of him. Why couldn't I just say, Darren, I really likes yer, boy. But it's out of order, en it, spressin yerself. People takes it the wrong way, like yer tryin to have illicit relations, like yer comin on too strong. Illicit. There's a fancy word for yer, ain't there? Illicit. Sometimes I used words like that with Jim. Illicit, I would say. An he would say, what the bleedin hell's wrong with you, Glory, swallowed a bleedin dictionary, have yer? An we'd have a good laugh.

But I likes words. I might not be able to write em down that good, but I likes to think about words I hear. Heard 'illicit' one night when the cops stopped me. Illicit dealins, they were accusin me of. Stupid fuckin bastards. I'd only stopped to talk to one of the young guys outta the drop-in. Locked him away, they did. Course, they didn't get nothin on me. Though sometimes it went through me head that it could be more comfy inside. An I might be able to learn sommat. Cos that's what I wanted, see. It was beginnin to burn at me, this thing I had, still has, with words. Specially when I saw Darren just at the age when he had a chance first time around. An I remembers how I fluffed it, buggered it all up, an wishes I could conquer it. So I thinks, well, the fuck, if they does get me hauled in on sommat, I could always spend me time learnin. Some of em end up real educated, you know. Look at Myra fuckin Hindley, BA in sommat or other, ain't she? Mind you, she was young when she went in. Whereas old meat like me, well, that takes a bit of stewin, don't it?

Anyhow, I'm gettin off the point, ain't I? Sweets, I was on bout. I dunno what the fuckin hell had got into me head thinkin bout givin the poor lad sweets anyway. Should have known better, the state *my* teeth are in. All black an rottin, those of em that are left that is. Can't bare the sight of meself in the mirror. One grin an it looks like the black fuckin hole of Calcutta. That an that grey hair with no shine to it. Beautiful that hair was once. Black. Masses an masses of thick glossy black curls. Not a bad looker all round when I was young. Cept me teeth were already goin. Should of looked after them better, shouldn't I?

Any rate, should of looked after them when I was workin in that toothpaste factory. Weren't exactly short of fuckin toothpaste, was I? You could get loads of cheap stuff in there. Not that I was on the factory floor, you understand. I was helpin in the canteen kitchens. An that was a sight for sore eyes. All these people comin in from makin tube after tube of toothpaste, comin an stuffin their faces with sticky puddings an all kinds of goo. You'd think it'd put them off, producin that sort of so-called healthy product, like. But it didn't. An I'll never forget one of the directors. She didn't usually come down to the canteen, but one day she did, I think there was some sort of business lunch goin on. All dolled up she was, hair in a french plait, posh dress, high heels, made up to the nines. An I'm standin beside her, deliverin a jug of water or sommat, when someone says sommat an she opens her gob to laugh, an all I can see is the fuckin fillins in her mouth. There, what d'you think of that? Fuckin director of a fuckin toothpaste factory with a mouth full of fillins. But that's life for yer, ain't it? Full of fuckin contradictions.

Got the fuckin sack from there, din't I. First job I had an I got into trouble. I weren't no trouble at school, like. Dead quiet, I was. Sat at the back, in me own little world. Didn't have many friends then neither. There was Louise. She weren't a bad pal. But then she got up the duff an left. Never saw no more of her after that. Someone said she got married eventually, moved up north. But I didn't do nothin like that. I sat at the back an dreamed. Didn't do no work. Couldn't see, for one thing. The words on the blackboard were a fog. An I got a headache strainin at it. An I got so far behind it would of bin impossible to catch up. Everythin seemed so difficult, an doin nothin was easy. Cos they couldn't be bothered with me. So we had an unspoken pact. They'd leave me alone, so long as I stayed quiet and didn't bother no-one. Which is exactly what I did. Good as gold. For four years.

Course Mum an Dad didn't say nothin. Mum didn't care about what I got up to at school. She just said I was homely. I'd make a good mother, she said. Kept me off when it suited her, to help catch up with housework an stuff. He of course didn't give a fuckin monkeys. He was too busy goin out to the pub an gettin assholed, comin back and beltin us about, or that other, of course.

I dunno how Sis got out of it really. Mum said she was the clever kid. Took up typin at school, she did, then left to do a secretarial course at college. Mum was dead proud of her. Sis got herself a job an a flat an started bringing Mum a bit of money now an then, sliding it into her hand when He weren't lookin. They had to be ever so careful. If he got his filthy hands on it he'd only fuckin drink it. An if he discovered that Mum had some money what he weren't told bout, then he'd have had sommat to say bout it. An he always spoke with his fists, I can tell you.

It was a Sunday mornin. Sometimes on a Sunday I used to put on me dress an go an sit in the cathedral at the back, have a word or two with our Lord. But I doesn't go that particular mornin cos I've arranged to meet Darren. So I has meself a fag an wanders over to the mews. There's ice on the pavements, an even after I've chucked me fag-end away, me breath's still comin out in clouds of smoke, the air's that cold.

I'm surprised to find the skip has gone. They must've taken it the night before, I guess. Strange time, it strikes me, but then these scrap blokes has a full schedule, don't they, hirin them out every bleedin minute that they can. Consumin what the consumers can't consume, as it were.

Anyhow, pop goes Jim's jacket, I thinks. Pity, but you can't win em all.

The yard's deserted. I looks up to see if Darren or his brother are peepin out their bedroom window. Not a twitch. They must be still asleep, I thinks. I hangs about for a bit, but there ain't no sign of him. Maybe I've got the time wrong. Bleedin heck, I chuckles to meself, it's like keepin a fuckin appointment. I'm sorry, Madam, but Master Darren is in a meeting with Mr Nod just now, shall I tell him you called...

So I decides to go home again, have meself a nice cuppa tea. Pity about the jacket.

It's then that I spots a plastic bag hidden in the corner where the two walls meets. I goes over an has a look. The bag's frozen to the pavement as I tries to pick it up to see what's in it. I tugs it away an leaves a jagged patch of white plastic frozen into the rough surface of the concrete. I knows by the feel of the bag what it is before I sees inside. It's like fuckin Christmas, en it? Feelin the presents an guessin what's in em before you looks. Not that I ever gets nothin for Christmas these days, but our Mum always did her best by Sis an me when we was kids. Though Christ knows where she got the readies from to pay for it all. Bein a barmaid wasn't exactly executive wages, an He drank all his.

An all the time I'm mutterin to meself, the little treasure, the little treasure, with a smile on me lips. An then I pulls out Jim's jacket, an holds it up, inspectin it like I was in a fuckin department store. Shall I take this one, I teases meself, or should I look round first an come back later?

But suddenly I can't wait to show Jim. So I rushes off, back through the park, trottin along with me head held high an me tail waggin like a bleedin dog, lookin this way an that, squintin an squinnyin, so's I won't miss seein him.

The little treasure, I'm sayin. Cos I can't believe that someone has done sommat special for Ol' Glory. The boy has actually looked the jacket out for me an even put it in a bag. Nobody ever does that sorta thing for an ol' gal like me. An there, Darren, a little seven year old what hardly knows me, has done just that. The little darlin.

Bloody hell, I thinks to meself, Jim had better bloody want it after all that! Still, if he don't want it, I'll have it, Yes, I shall bleedin have it.

I'm lookin for Jim all over. I even goes down by the gents, case he's down there, shouts in the door. But there ain't no reply, only some snooty geezer with a scowl on his face what says what right've the likes of you got to be round here, my good woman, though he never says nothin.

Oh well, I thinks, looks like me friends have deserted me this mornin, I'll go home for that cuppa.

The sun's shinin tho the air's bitter, an I'm feelin real good. I almost doesn't mind the bleak hollowness of the flat.

I've bought a bulb for Darren's Nana's lamp an I fits it in, arranges the lamp on a cardboard box for a table, tidies round a bit, tries to make the place look homely. Then I swills out a couple of mugs, fills one with tea an the other with cider, carries them into the front room, croonin a little ditty to meself. Things are lookin up, I thinks.

That's when the knock comes.

I goes over to the door, but I can't see no-one through the spy-hole so I guesses it's Darren come to apologise for not turnin up to our 'appointment'.

Fuckin hell, I has a shock when I sees him. He's got two black eyes an a swollen lip an one of his arms is in a sling. Blinkin heck, Darren, I says, what you done to yerself? I hustles him in an closes the door. He walks slow. Stiff as a bleedin broom.

'I ain't done nothin,' he says. 'I got told off for bein late home, that's all. I hate me Dad an I'm runnin away.'

It's then I notices the small rucksack on his back. What's this, I says. He takes the bag off his shoulders, opens it up.

'Got me toothbrush,' he says, real proud. 'An me jamas. An look, Glory, I brought you some books.'

He holds up three or four readin books. Pleased as punch, he is. Shows me the colourful covers. Kids an animals on the fronts. Then reads out the titles. *Red Hat, Yella Hat. Jim's Day Out.*

Zita at the Zoo. Yeah, still remembers em now, I does.

'*Jim's Day Out?*' I says. 'That reminds me, how d'you get that jacket?'

'I saw the men,' he says, 'they was just goin to load the skip an I said I had a friend what needed that jacket real bad, an one of em dug down an got it for me. Easy peasy.'

'You little bleedin charmer,' I says. Then blushes, cos for a minute I've forgotten me language. Believe it or not, I was tryin to make an effort that way, bout swearin an that.

'Sorry,' I says, 'I shouldn't say such words, should I?'

'Dad swears all the time,' Darren says. Then, all of a sudden he's real sullen. 'He swore a lot last night when I got in.'

'An did he really do that to yer?' I asks, pointin to his face and arm.

Darren sighs.

'Had to go to hospital. Mum told em I'd fallen down the stairs. Got back home in the middle of the night.' He pauses. 'Did you come this mornin?'

I nods.

'Sorry I didn't see yer.'

'Don't matter, me boy,' I says. 'Thanks for the jacket.'

'Hey,' he says, fear shadowin his face. 'You won't tell me Dad that you know he bashed me, will ya?'

'Course I won't,' I says, gentle like. 'Yer Dad an me's not exactly on speakin terms anyway, is we? Any case, I wouldn't tell if you didn't want me to.'

'Me Dad says if I tell anyone about it, he'll bash me over twice as hard.'

He's quiet for a minute, his little lip workin.

'Course, he's not goin to anyway, cos I ain't goin back.'

I'm thinkin hard, tryin to get me thoughts straight.

'An where do you think you're goin to exactly, young man?' I says at last.

He looks awkward, fingers the things out of his rucksack. Then looks up at me, with those bruised eyes.

'Can I live with you, Glory?' he says. Just like that. 'Can I live with you, Glory?'

Ain't that a bombshell an a half? Half-battered child shacks up with bag lady. That'd make a good headline, I says to him. Christ, if I'd known what was to come!

Course, I says no. I gives him a drink of water (I ain't got no squash or none of those fancy fizzy drinks they has today) an I manages to find a Rich Tea to give him. Then I says I'll go back with him. Bloody hell, I've got trouble on me hands then. He shouts an stamps his foot.

'No,' he says, 'I don't want to. I ain't never goin back.'

'Yes,' I says, 'you must.'

Though I've got tears in me eyes. I knows what it's like to face things, yer see.

'You can't stay here,' I says.

He bursts into tears.

'Then I'll go somewhere else,' he blubbers.

'Look, Darren,' I says, tryin to sound kind, but ready to crack inside, 'you'll really miss yer Mum.'

'Won't,' he balls. 'She takes no notice of me.' An yowls even louder.

'Look,' I says, gentle as I can, 'I'll take you home.'

It takes us a long time to get back to the yard. His legs are stiff. He says he can't see proper. It's beginnin to get dark. The street lights are comin on. Frost on the pavement twinkles beneath the car headlamps like fuckin Oxford Street at Christmas.

I hangs back near where the skip was.

'All right?' I asks. I feels awful. As if I was a grass, dobbin me pal in to the cops.

He nods, but he don't look at me.

I should of known. But I didn't, did I? Or maybe, I did know deep inside, but I was shuttin me eyes to it.

'See ya tomorra, if yer like,' I says.

'OK,' he says, non-committal like.

I takes it for sulks, but course, in reality, it was cos he had no bleedin intention of bein there the next day.

When I leaves him, he's walkin across the yard towards the door, an I'm thinkin to meself, poor little bleeder, who is there gonna protect him in the world? But I'm just like the rest of em. I walks away. I doesn't want to wait, to risk being seen. An I wanders away, slippin into the safety of the darkness.

When I gets back to the flat I sits in the dark, thinkin. I sees in me mind Darren's face, bruises the colour of them aubergines you gets on the market, an it's like lookin into the mirror at me own battered face all those years ago. Brings it back to me. Like vomit. Like a meal I never wanted to swallow in the first place. Digs it out of me past like psycho-fuckin-therapy. I doesn't want to recall those bloodshot eyes, the stitches above me lip. Nor the other neither. Yeah, that fuckin other. What other fuckin animal goes round maiming its own fuckin young? What bird pecks at its chick? What dog ruts with the pup fresh from the womb? Though when I comes to think of it, I remembers sommat Sis said once. Bout polar bear mothers havin to keep their young away from the adult males, case they eats em. Christ, what sort of fuckin world is this?

I'm gettin so fuckin upset with meself I has to go to the offie. That's bye-bye to nearly all that week's fuckin money. An what a fuckin week it was.

*   *   *

Is it you again? You with yer fuckin tape-recorder and yer note-pad. No offence like. Thought yer was comin yesterday actually. Disappointed I was when I found out it wasn't till today. Now, where had I got to? What's that? You bin wonderin if I ever seen Sis?

Well, the short answer (an the long answer for that matter) is no. Ain't seen her for years, I ain't. To begin with I kept up with her like, when I was working in that toothpaste factory an all, went to visit her in her la-de-da flat with her fuckin la-de-da fella. But even then, I always had the feelin I weren't good enough for her. Yer see, she were gettin on in the world an I were some guttersnipe what couldn't read a bleedin word. Yeah, I were an embarrassment.

That were one reason why she didn't want me around. Another was guilt, yer see. D'yer know anythin about guilt? It can do things to yer, yer know. An I reckon it did things to her. She'd left little sis behind, hadn't she? Got her exams, got out of that hell hole. Yeah, she'd put it all behind her and was gettin on in the world. And when she saw me, she felt guilty, cos she were succeeding where I weren't. An it made her feel bad. Plus she thought I might hate her for it. But I didn't. Tho I did envy her sommat rotten.

An there were another reason why she didn't want to keep up the acquaintance, as it were. She didn't want remindin of her roots. She wanted to forget it all. Forget about Him, bury it away beyond the deepest memories like mud beneath the coffin. She didn't need no cues for old memory lane from little sis.

Anyhow, I visited her less an less, an she never visited me at all. Then I got the sack from the toothpaste factory an was feelin mean with meself for a few months. Didn't want to see no-one for a bit. Then, when I decides to go along to see her, I discovers that she's moved away, left no forwardin address. She never bothered to notify me neither. I thinks of tryin Mum, but then that bastard was still there an I'd bin secret away from him that long I never wanted him knowin me whereabouts. Just sent cards Christmas an birthdays, me name scrawled on the bottom as best I could, an sent them through Sis.

Couldn't even write the fuckin envelope, could I? Yeah, up till I lost contact with her, I always heard about Mum through her. I think she used to sneak out of work an go an visit Mum durin the day so's to avoid Him, or else she visited late at night when he were down the boozer. Sis said that Mum never told Dad nothin bout us an what we was doin, just told him we'd disappeared. Which I did after that, I suppose, havin lost contact with Sis. Course, they'll both be dead now, won't they?

* * *

Funny, what with me talkin to yer bout Sis an that the other day, yer never gonna believe this but who should turn up here yesterday? It was like she heard us talkin through the fuckin ether.

Didn't recognise her at first like. For one, I weren't expectin her, an two, cos it's so many years since I saw her, she's changed. Yeah, she's aged. Still smart, like she always was, but she was lookin thin, an her face were grey and drawn, it were. Give me quite a shock, it did, when I finally realised who I were talkin to.

She'd seen me picture in the paper a few months ago, but she's been in hospital. Said she would of come earlier if she could of but was havin her fuckin tit cut off. Yeah, cancer. Though I'm surprised in a way she came at all, seein how I seems to be the black sheep of the family an all that. But then she'd been facin Ol' Nick, ain't she, an I think she's searchin to be at peace with everythin, even Ol' Glor.

SIS

Course, I never thought about going to see her, even when I found out where she was, because I'd also discovered what she'd gone and done. See, we were never that close, not even as little girls. Like I say, she was odd, a lazybones, and me, well, I buckled down and got on in the world, left my roots behind me. A plant can flourish even if it has started off on stony ground, long as it's transplanted and given a little TLC. Funnily enough it was Gerald that suggested I ought to go to see her. After all, she is your sister, he said, you're the only one she's got in the world. I don't know where he suddenly got all his compassion from, doling it out left, right and centre, or rather doling out *my* compassion. It must have touched a raw nerve with him some-where.

Yes, so when I got out of hospital and was feeling up to it, I went to see her. I guess there was an element of curiosity in there too. I just had to go and see if it really was our Glory. It was, of course. Though she was different from what I imagined. From what the papers said I expected to see a sort of monster. Someone always shouting and swearing and stuff. But she wasn't like that at all. No. She was calm and gentle and polite, though she did swear a bit. That's my Glory, I thought. Of course, it could have been the medication she was on that sub-dued her, made her much more 'amenable', let's say. All the same, I came away feeling quite affectionate towards her. I think I might go again. After all she's got no-one else, has she?

GLORIA

Next mornin when I gets up me head's splittin, it is, an I feels them walls closin in on me again. I has to get out. So I decides to take Jim's jacket an try to find him. Even if I doesn't, I thinks to meself, I'll enjoy the air, the walk.

I makes me way to the park. Sun's shinin. Air's crisp an fresh as an apple. I feels better already. There ain't no sign of Jim tho. Then I catches sight of Lester. He's an old geezer what lives beneath the railway bridge, he is. Bleedin heck, he don't arf pong. But he don't know where Jim is neither. Naa, Glory, he says, he's dead, ain't he? Bin dead fer years. Poor Ol' Lester. Off his rocker, he was.

Oh well, I sighs to meself, I'll go up the canal. See if Jim's up there. Leastways, someone up that way is bound to know where he's got to.

It's nice up the canal. A lot of it's old warehouses an that, but there's trees an all. No more leaves than Adam an Eve, they ain't. Just one or two hangin on like, as if they're tryin to win against time. But they're like us, ain't they? They got no choice in the matter. When they falls, they're dead.

Water's black as soot, it is. An in the distance there's factory smoke driftin across the sky like little carriages of white-grey cloud linked together. I remember it as if it were yesterday. Promised meself I'd paint a picture of it someday. Never have, like. Never have.

No sign of no-one up there though. Seemed like the whole fuckin world had deserted yours truly. Fuckin Marie-Celeste I'm thinkin, so I turns round an comes back down again. An then I'm just passin the paper shop when who does I see comin out but Jim.

'Hey, Jim,' I says, seein as he's nearly walkin right by, 'hey Jim, I bin lookin all over for yer, how yer doin?'

'Glory,' he nods.

Bloody hell, why do I fuckin bother, I thinks. He's still in one of his moods. Nonetheless, I takes the bull by the horns, reckons this might shake him out of it.

'Got yer jacket, Jim. The one I was tellin yer about. Me pal Darren got it for yer.'

An I'm right, this does perk him up a bit.

'Let's have a ganders then,' he says.

We walks along a bit, finds a bench to park our bums on, an I fishes out the jacket, hands it to him. He's runnin his heavy calloused hand across the thick tweed, gazin down at the small brown check, fingerin the heavy leather elbow patches. Anybody would think he was fuckin payin for the bleedin thing, he's bein that bloody fussy.

'It'll make me look like a bleedin school master, Glory,' he says, but he's lookin up at me, workin his lips in that way he has when he's pleased.

He stands up an takes off his overcoat. Underneath is a worn grey jumper, so thin yer can see his vest through it, yer can. Ragged at the sleeves an all, an too small, with stains down the front of it. He puts on the jacket, pulls the overcoat back on top of that. He looks bunged up like bleedin Humpty-Dumpty, but he says, 'Gor blimey, it ain't arf warm. Thanks, Glory, an thanks to your little pal.'

'Anyway, Jim,' I says, 'where you bin?'

'Hospital, Glory,' he says. 'Landed meself in the gutter like Nicholas fuckin Scott, din't I? Couldn't get no sense outta me, so they calls for an ambulance. I'd had a few jars like.'

He's tryin to button the overcoat up over the jacket, an I'm tryin not to smile at his efforts, cos what he's tellin me is serious like.

'Anyway, they told me what I knew all along. That I was all right. Couldn't bloody well leave me alone, could they? Eh? By the way,' he carries on, 'while I was stuck waitin in the bleedin corridor on one of those bleedin trolleys, I seen a little boy. Bout seven or eight he must have been. Bein pushed by, he was. His Mum an Dad were with him like. Right pair they looked. That boy's name was Darren an all. You'll be all right, Darren, his Ma was sayin. Darren, you'll be OK. Over an over again. Some sort of Northern accent, it was. Poor little bugger, didn't exactly look bleedin OK to me.'

'It'll be the same bleedin Darren, Jim,' I says, feelin sick inside. 'The same what got yer jacket for yer. He was in hospital. His Mum an Dad duffed him over, din't they.'

Jim sits back down on the bench. Gazes at his hands.

'Poor little sod,' he rumbles.

SIS

Of course, she always did swear quite a lot when she was a kid, though she didn't swear so much in front of adults. I think that it was another symptom of her illness, all that swearing. And it hasn't got any better as she's grown older from what I can gather. Language like that isn't really necessary though, is it?

GLORIA

We sits there for a while in silence, Jim an me. I offers him a
drink from me flask, but he says, no, Glory, I'll go buy a bottle.
By way of thanks, he says, for the jacket. He's feelin flush this
week.

'Been robbin the fuckin bank?' I says.

'Now, Glory,' he says. 'have a bit of respect. I been doin a
bit of work, ain't I. Brushin up leaves an stuff. Not that it's any
of your bleedin business,' he adds with a twinkle in his eye.

I sits on the bench while he trundles off to the offie. I'm gettin
cold an I'm wonderin if he would take it the wrong way if I
was to invite him back to the flat. At least it'd be out of the wind.

A van pulls up outside the newsagent's. The driver, a young
lad, chucks a bundle of papers out onto the pavement, makin a
thwack upon the hard surface, causin heads to turn. Then roars
off again. A man with a baldin head an a stomach what sticks
out further than St Paul's Cathedral comes out of the shop an
picks it up, carries it inside, comes out again presently an posts
up a new signboard with the headlines. I sits tryin to make it
out, what it says, like. I makes out a large B, an I'm wishin that
Darren had learned me to read already when I sees Jim comin
back.

'Hey, Jim, me eyes aren't what they used to be,' I says,
squintin an rubbin at me sockets with me fists, pretendin that
that would make a difference, 'what's that signboard say?'

I'm pointin over behind him, cos I knows Jim's a clever sod.
I knows he reads the papers an that, an I knows that a lot of years
previous he passed his exams. Sometimes I used to wonder
why he were in the state he were in. Yer thinks that someone
what's had an education as it were, would have more sense,
wouldn't yer? But yer see, yer forgets what he took all those
years. Yer forgets.

Jim's cranin his head forward towards the news-stand.

'My eyes ain't much cop neither, Glory,' he says, sighin an takin a step or two back along the pavement.

Then yells back at me, 'Young boy gone missin, it says.'

'There's always some poor devil goin bleedin missin,' I says, worryin more about me freezin toes at that minute. 'Listen,' I says, 'don't think I'm propositionin you or nothin but why doesn't we go along to my flat? I'm fuckin freezin.'

'Good idea,' says Jim. 'But, hold on, Glory.'

An he disappears into the newsagent's, appearin again a few minutes later with the paper tucked under his arm, an we trots along like the pals I s'pose we'd come to be. It's when we're goin up in the lift (yeah, it's bin fixed again) that he unfolds the paper to have a quick look at the front page. Suddenly he looks at me, real grim like.

'Christ, Glory,' he says, 'I think it might be your little lad.'

'What d'yer mean?' I says. But I knows already what he means.

'The one what's disappeared,' he's sayin. 'Listen to this.'

I peers over his shoulder pretendin to read along as he reads: 'Distraught parents of seven year old Darren Paley have appealed to the public for any information following the disappearance of their son last night.'

We steps out of the lift an I lets us into the flat. Me heart's thumpin, it is, me skin feels suddenly clammy. Cos I knew it was my Darren. I knew then what I ought to've known all along, that when I took him back that night, he never went in the bleedin house. Course he never fuckin went in.

We sits on the floor of me flat suppin whisky while I gets Jim to read the whole fuckin article over an over again, mutterin to him intermittent like that I must get round to seein an optician. But them sort of excuses're automatic like, things I bin sayin for years whenever I'm in a sticky situation far as readin or writin's concerned. But I ain't thinkin bout that, I'm thinkin bout what I'm hearin. An bleedin little Darren. An his bleedin awful Dad. An there's parts of the article, like 'worried parents' an 'we love our son an want him back' what really sticks in me throat. I washes them away with more of Jim's whisky.

I notices Jim starin at me.

'He'll come back, Glory. Don't you worry about it.'

'You doesn't understand, Jim,' I says. 'I was with him last night. I knows the little bugger. He back-tracked when I tried to take him home, scarpered as soon as me bleedin back was turned, didn't he? He won't come back now, Jim.'

'It ain't your bleedin fault, Glory,' he says, an pours some more whisky into me mug.

I sips it in silence all the while thinkin that yes, it is my fault, it is my bleedin fault. At last I murmurs, 'D'you think we could find him, Jim?'

But Jim don't reply. He's dropped off, what with the effect of the drink an that, his legs sprawled across the floor, his head leaned back against a heap of old clothes an newspapers.

Sleep is the last fuckin thing I wants though. Me, I has to think of sommat to do about that fuckin kid. Right, Glory, I says to meself, first thing to do is have a good feed. I ain't had nothin to eat all day, an it ain't no good, tryin to fink or do nothin on an empty stomach now, is it? As for Sleepin fuckin Beauty over there, I thinks, well, he'll need sommat when he wakes up an all.

Yet when I goes into the kitchen an rummages around for sommat, I realises after all that I can't face the thought of no grub. Cos I'm sick in me stomach with worry. I'd better have sommat, says one part of me. I can't, says the other. Anyhow, I'm just pullin out a couple of Ritz crackers from the box an beginnin to try to nibble at them, thinkin that anythin I shoves down is bound to want to come back up again, when there's a loud bashin at the door. Who the fuck can that be, I says. I glances at Jim who's stirrin with all the racket like, squintin up at me with a question on his face. There's another bash on the door. I goes over an spies through the peep-hole. There's no mistakin the dark uniform, the helmet.

'Fuckin pigs,' I whispers to Jim, movin as quiet as I can back away from the door.

They knocks again.

'Open up!' they're yellin from the outside. 'We know you're in there, Mrs Eden.'

I'm standin quite still. Me head's spinnin, light as a fuckin feather. I suddenly realises how fuckin pissed I am.

'Come on, Mrs Eden,' comes the deep voice from outside.

'What shall I do, Jim?' I whispers.

Jim shrugs.

'You ain't got nothin to hide, have you, Glory?' he says. 'We ain't done nothin wrong.'

'But I doesn't like em,' I says.

'They'll come back, Glory. They'll keep comin back till they gets what they want.'

I sighs deep.

I'm shakin as I turns the Yale, pulls open the door. A tall bobby with a moustache and a blond-haired WPC with her hair cut into a bob beneath that peaked hat is standin there.

'Yeah?' I says, real curt like.

They invites themselves in. Well, I ain't no option, has I? I can see their noses sniffin for trouble, goin twenty to the dozen like a couple of fuckin rabbits in front of a field of fuckin cabbages. Then they produces a picture of Darren.

'Seen this boy before?' they asks.

I hesitates. I can't think straight. I doesn't know whether to admit it or not.

'Seen his picture in the paper, ain't we, Glor?' Jim puts in, wagglin the news-sheet at the officers.

'That's right,' I says, cheered up by Jim's quick wits, 'I knew I'd seen him somewhere.'

'But you don't know him?' asks the WPC.

'Can't say that I does,' I says vaguely, hankerin after the last little drop in the whisky bottle standin on the floor besides Jim.

'Funny,' says the policeman, 'someone gave us a description

of a woman hangin around the yard outside his house over the past week or so. Checkin our records, it seems like that description led us to you.'

I says nothin.

'I'll ask you again,' says the copper, sighin impatient like, 'do you know this lad?'

'What if I does?' I says.

'If you *does*,' he says, takin the mickey out of me way of speakin, 'then I must warn you that you could be under suspicion.'

'Under suspicion?' I repeats, suddenly feelin confused by it all.

'For what?' Jim rumbles.

'Come on, Mrs Eden. Where is he?' says the WPC in a smarmy tone what really gets on me tit.

'How the fuck should I know?' I blurts, losin me rag all of a sudden. 'You an yer fuckin questions,' I yells. 'If I did bleedin know where the little bugger is, I'd be a lot fuckin happier than I am at the fuckin moment.'

'I should mind your language if I were you,' says the policeman, 'otherwise I'll have you for unruly behaviour.'

But I doesn't mind me language. I'm so fuckin upset, I'm goin fuckin wild, I am. An they ends by takin me down the copshop. Where they asks me all sorts else. They takes Jim too, but we doesn't see each other once we're there. Eventually, there ain't else for it, but I tells em bout Darren. Bout the skip, the way he turned up at me flat, uninvited like, an how I escorted him back to his door. I don't think they believed me, but anyhow, they lets me go late on. After they asks me to sign a bleedin statement, that is. What of course I can't make out. I sits there starin at it, tryin to figure out the words, an all they does is swim in front of me eyes till they goes a total blur. I thinks bout askin one of them buggers to read it to me, but then I'm in a hurry to get out of there, so in the end I just scratches me name at the bottom an hopes for the fuckin best.

They doesn't even give me a lift back to me flat, just turfs me out in the pourin bleedin rain, an I has to tramp all the way back across town. There's already rain in me shoes, then some posh car drives past an splashes a puddle all up me bleedin coat. Then, if that weren't enough, I gets caught up outside The George with a gang of fuckin youths. All larkin about drunk, they is. One of em pinches me bobble hat off me bleedin head, but I can't say nothin, cos I can see they're in the mood to show me the colour of me blood if I does, so I hurries on past as best I can without me flamin hat. Hopin to Christ they won't follow. Fuckin petrified I am.

Will Darren be like them when he grows up, I finds meself wonderin. If he grows up. Poor little bleeder, I thinks. What if he's already at the bottom of the fuckin canal?

When I finally gets back to me flat, I knows that the buggers have searched it, even before I've properly opened the bleedin door. The pigs, I mean. You can smell em, can't you, even tho there's not much sign of things bein outta place. The lav door's open – I always closes it – the clothes in the corner looks like they've been 'rearranged'. Only wastin their bleedin time, weren't they?

I makes meself a cuppa tea an sits down on the settee. I can't settle tho, I can't relax. It's like they're still here. Accusin me of sommat I haven't done. An I'm angry. Real angry. Cos I'm worried enough about Darren as it is, without bein accused of abductin the little bleeder. I wished he'd go home, wherever he was, I wished he'd stop bein so selfish an phone the police. Tho I knows in me heart it ain't nothin like selfishness, more a question of savin his own fuckin skin.

But it's the pigs what worries me. See, I been in trouble before – that's how they comes to have a record of me down at the copshop, ain't it? You guessed that, din't you? It weren't much like. Bit of shopliftin when I was hard-pressed, that's all. Needed a few things when I left Ray, din't I? Who's Ray? Blimey, that's a laugh. He was me husband.

Mrs Eden, you might well say, *you haven't mentioned your husband before.*

Yeah, well. Some things are better left dead an buried, ain't they. Not that he is dead an buried like. Tho he could be for all I knows. Fact is, I doesn't know where the ignorant bugger is, an I doesn't care. He were a blip in me life, one of many mistakes, and one of the few that I've managed to wriggle away from, relatively unscathed as it were. Course, even tho I seen what marriage meant for me own dear Ol' Mum, I were still fool enough to fall for all that fairy tale stuff, the prince what comes and rescues you an carries you off to success an riches. But it ain't bleedin like that, is it? It's never bleedin like that. We women has to stand on our own two feet if we wants sommat outta life. It ain't no use dependin on some miserable specimen of the opposite sex to sort yer out, cos they doesn't. All they wants is the business, if yer gets me meanin, an someone to do their fuckin washin. Isn't that right?

Anyway, I has a job in this posh restaurant, but I has to leave there when I leaves him. I finds a bed-sit and goes down the social. They keeps askin the same fuckin questions over an over again like a fuckin record-player. Mrs Eden, they says, what are your reasons for giving up your job at La Cigale? Anyway, they won't pay out, an I ain't got nothin. I'm starvin, I am. So I helps meself a little bit. From the local supermarket like. An at first it works, don't it? Buy some, nick some. Easy fuckin peasy. Could pick up whatever I fuckin fancied for tea. Then they goes an catches me.

Anyhow, I gets probation for that, don't I, first bloody offence an all that. As well as bein extenuatin circumstances, I thinks they calls it. Life is full of extenuatin circumstances, ain't it? Sometimes I thinks life is one long fuckin extenuatin circumstance.

Lynne, her name was. Me probation officer, that is. Nice girl. Sympathetic like. Helped me get a better place an got me in the queue for me flat. Even helped me find a job down the bottle factory. But that was when me Trouble began.

Yeah, I starts to feel real low. I've lost contact with me family, made a hash of me marriage, an I suddenly realises that I'm all alone. Then I starts gettin these dizzy turns. I'm not on probation no more, an I doesn't seem to have made no new friends at the bottle factory. There's no-one to talk to, is there? Everyone around me seems tied up with their own bleedin business. To them I'm just funny Ol' Gloria from work what keeps herself to herself.

To begin with, I starts buyin meself a bit of booze on me way home, so's I can cheer meself up. Then I finds the dizziness is botherin me at work an all, so I starts fillin a little flask to take with me, help me through the day like. Has a little tipple at tea-break, an lunch. Secret like. Usually in the lavs.

But it's all gettin a bit pricey, an I begins to wonder if I could help meself to a bottle or two from the offie. Then I thinks, naa, get a grip, Glory, all you has to do is cut down a bit. But then I thinks I deserves some pleasure in life.

An then Fate deals a blow. They smells it on me breath. Boss calls me into his office, like, says he's reason to believe I've bin drinkin on the premises. It's not on, he says, drinkin an bein in charge of machinery, it's dangerous. An he issues me a warnin. If he catches me again, he says, he'll have to relieve me of me duties. Christ hell, I thinks, is life worth fuckin livin. The next week I'm out on me ear.

I goes down the social, but course, they ain't gonna pay nothin. Me rent's due an I ain't got a bean. The landlord boots me out. Comes round, he does, accompanied by a big bloke with more tattoos on his arms than there's patterns on Laura Ashley wallpaper, an a fuckin great Rottweiler. Says he don't want my sort round on his property. That's the type of thing people says to yer, yer know. Your sort. Clumps yer together with every Tom, Dick an Harry. What does it mean, your sort?

So I gathers up me few possessions in a hold-all an mooches round the streets for a few weeks. First time in me life I had nowhere to go. I sleeps in bus-shelters, doorways, that kinda thing. Sometimes yer gets moved on by the police. Sometimes they leaves yer alone. It weren't winter, thank Christ. Tho it were cold enough at night. A tipple helps to keep yer warm, dulls yer senses. Yeah, a nice spot of sommat. If you can get it. Sometimes yer can beg a few pennies. You walks along with yer hand out, palm flat to the sky, tryin to look pathetic. Some of em, they paints a stick white an walks along with their peepers almost closed, cunnin buggers. They says it works, yer know.

I'm still gettin these dizzy spells. Annoys me, it do, not feelin on top of things, as it were. Makes me feel wound up inside. An still I'm lonely as hell. An the more worse I feels, the more difficult it is to talk to people. Even the girl at the check-out, the bus conductor. They looks at yer as if they doesn't wanna know, an it shakes yer confidence, it do, so yer don't say nothin, an if yer does, it all comes out wrong. Then yer gets cross, an it seems like it's all their fuckin fault, so yer swears at em. Then yer gets into fuckin trouble. Next thing yer knows, yer down the fuckin lock-up, spendin the night behind bars.

I doesn't get no other job after the bottle factory, tho I tries. I gets me flat tho, the one what Lynne had put me down for, then the social starts payin up, an I starts tryin to make sense of me life again. But I'm feelin bad in meself. I sees women same age as me, in their twenties, pushin pushchairs, their little babies all done up in woollies, their pink little faces an their little snub noses pokin out. I sees little girls kneelin up on the seats, facin me on the bus, smilin. I sees boys in the park on winter days kickin a ball around in their shirt sleeves, mud pasted to their knees. An I feels envy. An I thinks, why can't *I* have a bloke to look after me, a kid or two, a room with a carpet an a telly?

But I knows why not. An it makes me angry. It was Him, weren't it? He ruined me, he did. An that's why I ain't never had no proper life. An the more I thought about it, the more I hated him. D'yer know, I could almost of gone back an murdered him. Really, I mean murdered. In cold fuckin blood. Stabbed him to death. Stead, I went down hill. Persecuted by me own fuckin thoughts. Drinkin whatever I could lay me hands on. Till I ends up in hospital with slashed fuckin wrists. Bandages me up an puts me under a doctor, they does. Who gives me a load of fuckin pills to swallow.

When I comes out I decides I'm gonna get a grip, sort a life out for meself. An that's what I did, in a way. Passed the time with me little hobbies. Collectin things an that. Seein what I could pick up from skips, nosin in bins. That sorta thing. Sometimes I'd sell the odd thing I found for scrap. An the years peeled away, like layers of onion, each fresh layer lookin just the same as the layer before, only there's less an less of it – an yer uses it quicker an quicker. But then Darren comes along, an it's all change. All fuckin change.

Yeah, so I'm back at the flat, en't I? Me head's sizzlin with all the happenins. An most of all I'm feelin guilty that I didn't watch Darren go through his front door. Guilt that I was too fuckin chicken to hand him back to his Mum in person like, explain what had happened. I could of taken the risk that she would of believed me, even if she hadn't fuckin thanked me for it. Then again, what would she of done to little Darren? Even if she had welcomed him in, I couldn't see his fuckin Dad offerin no kind words. Then I starts feelin guilty about not keepin Darren in me flat, gettin him settled down to sleep, then sneakin out an ringin the authorities like. See, I made a balls up, din't I? I was scared to approach the police, his mother, social workers, whatever. An also I was afraid to use the fuckin phone. Couldn't use the fuckin telephone directory. Only thing I could fuckin dial was 999. I had a chance to do sommat the right way, an I went an did it fuckin wrong, din't I? An there an then I resolves not to fuck it up again. If I gets a second chance, I thinks to meself, I'll show a bit of fuckin responsibility.

Me thoughts turn to Jim. I guesses he's got back safe from the nick. But I'm pissed off cos I thinks that nothin'll tempt him round here again. Not in a long while. Jim ain't one for hangin around trouble if he can help it, I thinks.

At long last I settles down for a bit of shut-eye. Me head's still spinnin, it is. What with tiredness, booze an worry. But I falls to sleep anyhow. An next day when I wakes, the winter sun is already shinin its ivory rays from the south.

Shit, I says to meself when I wakes up an sees the sun shinin in, that's a whole fuckin mornin I could of bin lookin for Darren. But then I rolls over an thinks why the hell should I bother? Blasted kid's probably turned up again by now. Yeah, he'll be safe home, I was thinkin. But then I considers the word 'safe'. It ain't exactly accurate now, is it? An I thinks, maybe he's better off not goin home, but that makes me start worryin about all them evil things out in the world ready to prey on kids what've run away from home.

An I'm lyin there tossin an turnin, thinkin that if Darren is at home by now, how the bleedin hell am I gonna find out? Will I have to trail all the bleedin way down the nick just to find out if he is or if he ain't?

I can't stay in me bed a minute longer, I gets up an makes a cuppa tea. The flat's cold, it is. The wind's whistlin through the frenchie like it was goin through a fuckin tunnel. Rain's gobbin at the panes. By Christ, I thinks to meself, that little tike'll know all about it if he's out in this.

There's only one thing for it. I pulls on me coat, an lines me shoes with fresh newspaper. Then I sets off. I'm apprehensive bout goin, I am. What if they detains me again? I saunters along, pretendin to meself it ain't urgent, it ain't none of me business. I stops in a bus shelter, to get out of the rain for a few moments. But the more the rain lashes against the glass, the more I comes to think it is me bleedin business, an off I hurries once more.

'Well, Mrs Eden,' says the constable on duty, 'got some information for us, have we?'

His head's goin up an down knowingly like one of them fuckin noddin dogs you gets in cars. His fingers are tappin lightly on the counter.

'No,' I says, sarcastic like, 'we ain't got no bleedin nothin. I wants you to tell me sommat.'

An I asks if he's got any news about Darren. The police constable looks at me with a smirk.

'Not allowed to divulge any information,' he says, his tongue pushin out the side of his cheek like a bleedin hamster.

'Look here, you arsehole,' I says, losin me rag.

'Ah, ah, ah,' he interrupts, waggin his finger at me as if I was a bleedin kid, 'language can get you into trouble.'

I lets out a puff of air.

'Listen,' I says, tryin to curb me temper, 'I just wants to know if I should be lookin for that kid or not.'

He starts to laugh.

'Very good, Mrs Eden. Very funny! What do you think the likes of you can do that a full police team complete with tracker dogs can't manage? That's what I'd like to know!'

The phone's ringin an he's pickin it up an answerin it. Which is just as well. Otherwise I might of said sommat I would of regretted. Instead, I charges out of the police station in a ragin fury an goes stormin up towards the canal.

The walkin begins to calm me. At least, I thinks to meself, that copper as good as told me that Darren still has not been found. All I knows now is that I've got to bloody well find him first.

Course, I thinks, Darren could be up in one of those shacks that are part of the moorings for the houseboats. I'll go an have a sniff about there. I walks along, softly callin his name, case he's hidin. But there's no reply. Next thing I knows I'm approachin a team of coppers combin the bank. There's a police-boat too, with divers. I turns me head away from em. I can't bloody look, can I? I doesn't wanna see, case his poor sodden body is at that very moment bein lifted from the water.

I passes em all. They doesn't say nothin, tho I can see me presence doesn't go unnoticed. They've got dogs with em. I'm bleedin petrified of the things, noses to the ground, tuggin at their leads like great flamin monsters. I thinks, what if they can smell Darren on me? They'll be leapin up an knockin me into the fuckin canal. I hurries on. Past the warehouse an on to the allotments, whisperin to the sheds. Some geezer fiddlin about with a bunch of onions looks at me funny, but I carries on. Darren, I whispers, it's Glory. Darren, mate, it's Glory. But nothin.

Last, I decides to go home. The long way round. Not back along the towpath past those fuckin cops. By the time I gets to me block, me feet are achin me fuckin socks off.

But it weren't just me feet that were achin. It were me fuckin heart what was really hurtin. I felt like without little Darren nothin weren't worthwhile no more, nothin in this bleedin world. What sort of life has that kid had, I was thinkin to meself. An what can I do about it? I felt so fuckin powerless. An I was thinkin, how many other bleeders are there? Sufferin like him. Sufferin like I did. Eh? Answer me that.

An I'm enterin the block, gettin in the lift, an I can feel meself wantin to blubber. Yeah. I wants to cry an cry an cry. Cos I thinks, this time me heart is well an truly breakin. I steps out the lift an pushes through the fire doors into the corridor, an who does I see sittin in the gloom, back up against me door, long legs splayed out across the floor, but Jim.

'Where the bleedin heck've you bin?' he rumbles.

'Lookin for Darren,' I says, wipin the tears out the way with me sleeve. 'Didn't expect to see you here. Thought you wouldn't be seen within a mile of the bleedin place after yesterday.'

He don't reply. Then he says, 'I think I knows where that lad of yours is.'

Me heart lands in me mouth.

'Yer'd better come in,' I says. An I quickly unlocks the door an ushers him inside.

'Where is he?' I asks. 'Is he still alive?'

'Course he's bleedin alive,' says Jim. 'Typical bleedin woman, always thinkin the worst.'

'All right, all right,' I says, impatient like, 'get on with it. Where is he?'

'Course, it might not be him,' says Jim, lightin up a fag, nearly drivin me demented with his bloody slowness, 'but I'm pretty sure he matched the photo in the paper.'

'And?' I says, seethin.

Jim takes a drag.

'Well, Glory,' he says at last, 'you know I sometimes goes down to the railway station for me fags from the machine when places're closed an that?'

I nods.

'Well, I was down there for me fags an decides to go to the gents. Well, who's in there but this little lad, bit scruffy like, little rucksack on his back. Cleanin his fuckin teeth, he is. When he looks up I gets a good look at his face in the mirror, an I thinks, ay ay, it's him all right.'

'An did you say sommat to him?' I asks.

'What d'you bleedin think, Glory?' says Jim, impatient like. 'Get real. If an old geezer like me started talkin to him, he'd be off like the clappers.'

'So where did he go, Jim?' I asks, wantin to know everythin at once. 'Was he down there to catch a train?'

'Well,' says Jim slowly, 'he went out of the lavs, an after a moment or two, I follows. I sees him at the other end of the platform, standin there, back in the shadows a bit, as if he's waitin to get on a train. But two trains come in an he don't get on either. I think he was just watchin them. Yer know, like kids do. Then two cops come strollin down the platform, an when I turns me head back to see what young Darren's doin, he ain't nowhere to be seen.'

'So, where d'yer think he went?' I asks.

'I reckons he's hangin out down there somewhere – there's sheds, old railway carriages – I wouldn't be surprised if he didn't break into one of those, I wouldn't.'

I scrambles up from where I've bin sittin on the floor, listenin.

'Come on, Jim, we've gotta go out.'

He screws his face up into a snarl.

'Bleedin heck, Glory,' he says, indignant like, 'you ain't draggin me all the way down where I just come from, are yer?'

'Jim,' I says, 'this could be a matter of life an death.'

He groans as he gets to his feet.

'Bleedin heck, Glory,' he repeats as I tugs him outta the flat an slams the door.

It's gettin late. The sky's soupy with darkness; the street lights shine up into it, sittin on the murkiness like a thick yellow scum. An as we walks there's pockets of fog driftin in around us, like ghosts. I doesn't mind tho. I'm thinkin it could be useful in our search. Hide us, like.

First stop is the station itself. Jim checks the gents, just in case, while I peeks in the waitin rooms. Not that I thinks Darren'll be in there. I knows he's got more sense than to hang around the obvious places.

Then we walks along the platform, but there's a railwayman at the end, so we does an about turn – not too obvious like – an cuts up along the road till we gets to the railway bridge. Then we has to climb over this wire fence. That must of bin a sight! Wrigglin an swayin about on these wires, I was, like some sorta fuckin trapeze artist, tryin to get me leg over an stay steady while I tries to swing the other one towards it. Course, Jim's gettin over real easy what with his long legs an all. Rather, he is until he miscalculates the length of his bleedin overcoat. Just as he's jumpin down there's a great rippin sound where he catches one end of it on the barbed wire, lettin out a string of curses as he stumbles to the ground.

'Shhh!' I hisses.

'Torn me bleedin coat, en't I?' he says crossly. 'I'll be billin your bleedin Darren for a new one.'

'He already got you a jacket,' I whispers back, good-natured like, 'what more d'you fuckin want?'

He grunts, surprisingly good-humoured. In a strange kind of way, we're both enjoyin ourselves, even tho I'm worried to death about Darren an that. See, I hadn't ever done nothin as excitin as that in all me life. Nor Jim neither, I don't think.

Anyhow, I'm wobblin over the fence after Jim an his torn coat, thinkin that the whole fuckin thing is gonna collapse with all me weight, an the swingin about on it an that, thinkin that I'm gonna go sprawlin on me face, me body plaited with fuckin barbed wire. But at last I gets over. Pitch, it is.

'Goes down now, Glory,' whispers Jim. 'You OK?'

I says that I am, though I ain't feelin too certain.

An then suddenly I feel him fumblin for me hand with his.

'We'll go down together,' he rumbles.

I felt strange holdin his hand like that. Two fuckin grown-ups like two little nippers. It had been a long time since I'd touched someone, since someone had touched me. With care, that is. Not a shove from a cop, not a 'move-along-please' or 'get-in-there-you-bastard', not a push from the likes of me Dad or Ray, meanin 'I'm-gonna-get-the-goods-whether-you-likes-it-or-not'. No. Just a touch in innocence. In companionship. In common purpose. In lookin after each other.

Anyhow, we're scramblin down this bank, we are, hand in hand, in the pitch black, away from the bridge when we hears the rumblin of a fuckin locomotive comin towards us. We has to charge back like dogs, press up against the side of the bridge, crouchin behind some sorta bush, hopin nobody will bleedin see us, while it goes past.

When it's gone we gets up, but it's that bleedin muddy I slips right back down again sprawlin out onto me front, endin up with me nose stuffed right into the middle of this fuckin bush. I lies there for a minute, feelin exhausted. My Christ, I thinks to meself, what the fuck am I doin here. But the smell of the cold, damp air, and the peppery, vinegary yet sweet scent of rottin leaves sizzles in me head like a tonic, an somehow, I takes heart.

'I've heard of bein next to nature,' I says to Jim, extractin meself from the branches an thorns what tug at me coat, 'but this is fuckin ridiculous.'

An I hears Jim chortlin in the darkness.

Once again Jim an me holds hands as we scrambles down the bank an walks along the side of the track, keepin our focus on the fog-blurred station lights. As we approaches, Jim says that he reckons Darren'll be over the other side if he's anywhere, an that we oughta cross the line.

'Christ, Jim,' I says, 'we're not gonna be fuckin electrocuted, are we?'

But then all of a sudden we realises we've arrived at a level crossin just before the station.

'Here,' says Jim, 'we'll go across here.'

So across we trundles, an forks up besides the track on the other side. We can see beneath the station lights the tracks splayin out like huge fingers from the palm, the tips disappearin into the fog. Over to the left is some sheds. We goes behind them. It's dark again, an I keeps trippin on stones, clumps of weeds and what I imagines must of bin disused sleepers. There's a corrugated lean-to joined to one of the bigger sheds. Jim lets go me hand an fumbles in his pocket for a match, strikes it up an for a few seconds we can see inside the bit of shed. On the floor there's a few rotten clothes draped on top of a half-shredded black bin liner. As far as I could see, that is. Nothin more.

'Look, Glory,' Jim says. 'I reckon he's been sleepin here. There's a fresh crisp packet, look, an a coke can.'

'Could be any bugger,' I says.

'Yeah, but it ain't likely,' says Jim. 'This is where Ol' Codger died. Most of us that knows keeps away from this spot. The person that's been here'll be someone new, I bet.'

The light from the match has long since died, an we're standin in the dark. We reckons that Darren's been here one or two nights, but it seems like he's gone now. Nevertheless, we has a bit more of a sniff around, wanderin about callin his name in the lowest of whispers. But all we hears is the occasional sound from the station, the sharp bark of a railwayman to one of his mates, another whistlin, a train comin in, the sound of traffic from town, sounds wrapped an muffled in tissue-paper fog.

Gloomily we makes our way back to the railway crossin, walkin out on to the road this time, bold as brass. Then we trudges back towards town, all the excitement of earlier havin soaked away, leavin our spirits dry. Jim leaves me at the corner where the road to his block branches off away from the road leadin to mine.

'I'll come see you in the mornin, Glory,' he says.

'OK, Jim,' I replies, but inside I doesn't believe him, cos I knows when he gets home he'll start on the whisky, an he'll probably still be drunk in the mornin.

For a moment I stands watchin as his stoopin figure disappears into the thick yellow mist, then I continues on me way. I'm really tired, me eyes are stingin, me legs're like lead. The lift is still workin, surprise surprise, so I gets in it, tho as a rule I doesn't use it at night. Yer never knows who you might get stuck in it with, do yer?

An it's just as I'm pushin open the fire-door into the corridor that a movement catches the corner of me eye   Christ, I thinks, me heart takin a leap into me mouth, there's someone lurkin, who the fuck… ? But when I steps towards me door, there ain't no sign of no-one, an I thinks I must of imagined it. Probably after all that fog dancin before me eyes. Still, I can't quite shake off an unpleasant feelin of bein watched. Christ, Glory, I shivers to meself, yer'd better get in bloody quick, could be some mad mugger or rapist. An I'm workin meself up into a lather bigger than what you gets on top of a pint of Guinness, fumblin for me key, which, Christ, ain't in the pocket I usually keeps it in. At last I finds it, but I can't get the fuckin key in the lock, me hands are shakin that fuckin much, an then I hears footsteps behind me, an I'm sayin to meself, Glory just get that fuckin door open, an I feels like I'm gonna shit meself, an I'm just gettin in an ready to slam the door behind me when this fuckin little voice comes pipin out the gloom. Hello Glory.

Christ, I could of killed the little bleeder.

'Darren!' Yelps it, I does, like a frightened pup. 'Darren, you scared the livin daylights outta me, you did.'

But while I'm sayin it, I'm fuckin smilin, no, I'm laughin, laughin I am. An I'm huggin the little lad to me, an he's huggin me.

'Am I glad to see you,' I says, still gigglin, makin way for him to go through the door into the flat.

I turns Darren's Nana's lamp on, looks him up an down. Christ, he's in a state. His clothes are filthy an he smells like a fuckin sewer.

'Where you bin sleepin?' I says. 'An look, yer filthy.'

'Oh, I've been washin me face and cleanin me teeth regular, Glory,' he says, barin a row of white teeth.

'I knows,' I says.

His little face looks puzzled for a minute.

'How d'yer know?' he asks.

'Friend of mine saw you down the station lavs.'

He don't say nothin.

'I see Nana's lamp's still workin,' he says.

'Hey,' I says, 'you could do wiv a hair wash.'

An I goes an switches on the mersion. Blow the lecky bill, I thinks, this is an emergency.

While we're waitin for the hot water, I gives him a drink an a Rich Tea. He gollops em down. (That's a good word, ain't it? Gollops.) He gollops em down at such a rate that I realises how hungry the boy is, an I knows I'm gonna have to go out an buy him sommat decent.

'Got any money?' I asks.

He shakes his head.

'Spent it all,' he says.

I doesn't want to dip into it, but I has a little bit put aside for emergencies. I tells Darren to stay put in the sittin room an goes into the bedroom, rakes an old jam jar from amongst the dust an clutter underneath the bed. I wipes it down with me sleeve an opens it up. There's a five pound note an some coins. I ain't sure

how much, cos I ain't much good at countin, but I knows I've got
enough to do a bit of shoppin. How does I manage, shoppin, yer
askin. Well, as a rule, I just hands me purse over to the cashier
an they takes what they needs. I know that's very trustin of me,
an maybe I shouldn't do it. But then what else can a body do?

'You all right here on yer own,' I asks, goin back into the
front room, 'while I goes out to buy sommat to eat?'

Me little guest nods, picks up his glass an drains the last drop
from it.

'You're dry as a bone, ain't you,' I says, an fetches him
another glass of water.

An I leaves him drinkin it while I goes out to the corner
shop. Open all hours it is. I buys a sliced white loaf an a tin of
beans, some yoghurts, a small packet of cornflakes an some
milk for breakfast, a small bar of soap cos I ain't in the habit of
usin soap, an another light bulb to light the place up a bit better. Coo, I thinks, feelin the weight of the bag as I lifts it from
the counter, this lot'll keep him goin. An I skedaddles back to
the flat as quick as I can. Doesn't want him disappearin off
nowhere again. No.

I'm worryin that I oughta of called on Jim to tell him that
Darren has turned up, but I hasn't got time to go along to his
flat, so I decides that it'll have to wait till mornin. Any case, I
thinks, he'll probably be out of it an won't remember that I'd bin.

When I gets in, first thing I does is put the light bulb in the
bedroom socket. Darren switches it on to see if it works while
I'm climbin down. There ain't no lamp shade, course, so it
nearly blinds the pair of us, lookin at it.

'Like bleedin Blackpool illuminations,' I says, forgettin me
language.

'Yeah,' says Darren, grinnin. Then, he asks, 'Can I have my
bath in the dark?'

'Yer ain't got no choice, me boy,' I says.

'Cool!' he says, real excited at the prospect.

'I hope not,' I says, worryin about me lecky bill again.

While Darren's in the bath, I gets his tea, an when he's eaten an I've cleared the things into the kitchen, I comes back into the front room an says right, Darren, now yer fed an watered, we has to decide what yer gonna do. But it's too late, cos he's curled up on the settee fast asleep. I drags off the couple of blankets what I has on me bed an covers him up as best I can. Sommat's comin back to me, sommat what I heard on the radio about hypothermia or sommat – it's the first thing they checks for if yer've been stuck up a mountain or what, an they rescues yer, yer know. Checks to see if yer warm enough, wraps yer up in blankets, they does. Learns lots of things from the radio, yer does. Lots of interestin things. Yeh.

Anyhow, with pictures before me eyes of him fuckin dyin of cold overnight, I covers him up, an realisin how tired I am meself, I goes an lies down on me bed, usin me overcoat as a blanket. Cos I ain't got no more covers, see. It's fuckin freezin, it is. I has a slug or two from me flask, to warm me up, like. Blasted kid, I curses, but I'm feelin real happy inside, an nods off quick as a wink.

Next mornin when I wakes up, Darren's already up. He's pushed the bottles all to one end an he's tryin to set the table for breakfast, bless 'im. An he ain't arf lookin puzzled about it all.

'I can't find nothin,' he says.

'That's cos I ain't got nothin,' I chuckles, 'but it's good of yer to try.'

'I always does it at home,' he says. 'That's my job.'

'While we're on the subject of home,' I says, findin a bowl for Darren an pourin out some cornflakes, passin him it an the milk, 'we've got sommat to sort out.'

I looks at him serious like an a little frown puckers his eyebrows.

'I ain't goin back, if that's what you mean,' he says.

'Darren,' I says, 'you can't stay here.'

The words echo in me head. I knows I said em last week, an I remembers his tears. Now, again, his eyes fill, but he ain't so submissive.

'Why can't I?' he yells all of a sudden, real angry like.

'Shhh,' I says, 'yer'll wake the babies.'

'What babies?' he demands, real aggressive like.

I shrugs.

'Dunno,' I says. 'Babies in the vicinity. Me Mum used to say it to shut us up when we was kids.'

He looks at me as if I'm fuckin gaga, he does, but he shovels some cornflakes into his gob an don't say nothin.

'I'm serious, Darren,' I continues, 'Your Mum an Dad'll be worried sick about yer. There's cops down dredgin the canal lookin for yer body, there's cops down the railway station, there's cops everywhere. You has to go back.'

He sits silent, his breakfast only half eaten, idly picks a cornflake outta the milk an pops it in his mouth.

'I'll take yer back after breakfast,' I says.

'No,' he shouts, an flings his bowl across the table. Milk runs from the mush of cornflakes an drips on to the floor.

Course, I'm fuckin furious. I sees me hard-saved money drippin down in that milk. All that fuckin effort, searchin up the canal, down the station, all over the fuckin place, goin down the fuckin nick, an that's the thanks yer gets for it. I'm blind with anger. An I'm standin there, facin him across the table, stormin, an he's howlin his fuckin willy off in fuckin stereo, an all of a sudden I catches meself on an I thinks this baby has only been outta the womb seven years an I've bin out over fifty, an he's still learnin, an all he's learnin right now is it's OK for adults to holler out a whole set of swear words, an I stops in me tracks. Dead. An I goes over to him an I says in a quiet voice, I'm sorry.

It was a long time since I had said those words to anyone (tho I says them often enough now, I reckons). Mind you, there had never bin no-one worth sayin them to. Not up till then.

I'm sorry, I says. An he stops hollerin, instant like. An he's gawpin at me in amazement. Silent as a penny dropped in a fountain. I doesn't think no-one's ever said sorry to him neither. An then we just hugs each other. For a long time.

'I can't let yer stay here,' I groans in a half-hearted manner, strokin his hair with me rough old hand.

'I don't wanna go home,' he says in a sorrowful voice. Then adds, stronger like, 'If you takes me home, Glory, I'll run away again.'

'Don't I believe it,' I mutters to meself.

I makes meself a cuppa an clears up the mess.

'If you lets me stay,' Darren says at last, 'I'll learn you to read.'

'There's an offer an a half,' I says.

But I doesn't make up me mind straight away. Rather, I says I'll think about it. Besides, I wants to wait an see what Jim's got to say about it all.

By late mornin seein as Jim ain't turned up, I tells Darren that I'm goin out to look for him. I leaves him with strict instructions not to open the door to no-one, an trundles off down the lift an out the block. The sky's blue as Delft, it is, white frost coats the shadier pavements an verges where the sun ain't reached, the air's still as a church. Thank you, God, I says under me breath, thank you that he's still with us, bless his little soul. It ain't that I'm particular religious, it's just that I was grateful to the world that sommat in this life had gone right for a change, cos Christ, it ain't often that it does.

I turns to go towards Jim's block, but then I notices that familiar figure comin towards me.

'I was just comin to hoick yer out, Jim,' I says when he's caught up with me.

'I s'pose yer didn't think I'd come, did ya, doubtin bleedin Thomas,' he grumbles, good-humoured like.

'Guess who's turned up?' I says, all excited.

'Has he now?' says Jim, his jaw droppin. Then in that teasin tone, 'I never knew the Duke of Edinburgh was a personal friend of yours.'

'Jim,' I says, impatient, 'you know who the bleedin heck I means.'

'We goin up to see the little sod, then?'

An Jim starts walkin towards the main entrance to our flats, turnin his head an winkin at me, his head cocked like one of them fuckin Springer Spaniels.

We goes up an lets ourselves in. Darren's sittin there with his readin books all spread out across the floor, looks a bit frightened like when he sees Jim.

'It's all right,' I says. 'This is me friend Jim, the one what you got the jacket for. Don't you recognise it?'

I pulls the corner of Jim's overcoat open to expose the jacket underneath. Darren gives a little smile. Then Jim goes over an offers Darren his hand.

'Pleased to meet you, young man,' he rumbles.

I ain't never seen Jim so outgoing before. Sometimes he's hard pushed to spare two words together for the sake of talkin. But somehow I has the feelin that things is changin, that this is sommat he wants to be part of.

'I'm goin to learn Glory to read,' Darren tells Jim proudly, gazin down at his books.

'Are you now?' says Jim. 'I never knew our Glory didn't know how to.'

An I feels me face colourin up. I'm so embarrassed that it's come out like this, but more than that, embarrassed cos I realises by his tone that Jim knew all along, saw through all the pretendin.

It's absurd but I can't just come out an admit it now, I can't admit that I've been pretendin to him, so I flusters a bit, an says, 'Well – thought me spellins could do with a bit of brushin up – type of thing…'

An Darren's lookin up at me perplexed like, an Jim's sayin, very good, very good, in a nudgin sort of way, playin along, lettin me off the hook like.

Jim squats down in front of Darren, his great hunkin bulk castin a shadow over Darren's books. I can see Darren's still afraid of him, but he don't move, an Jim, gentle as a lamb, says, 'You gonna go back to your Mummy?'

Darren fixes his gaze on Jim's face. Real square an bold.

'No,' he says, 'I'm stayin here.'

Jim rises up again.

'In that case, Glor,' he says, glancin appraisin like around the flat, 'if you don't mind me sayin, I think we should make the place a bit more comfy for the lad.'

'In that case,' I says, irritable (an I puts on this hoity-toity voice), 'I'll just pop down to Habitat to order one or two things, put it on the account.'

Jim grins, exposin a row of rotten teeth.

'Serious, Glor,' he says. 'You just wait an see, you'll be surprised what I can pick up to improve things a bit.'

'We ain't housin the bleedin Royal Family yer know,' I says, edgin more humour into me voice.

Jim turns to go.

'Can I come?' Darren pipes up, goin up to Jim.

I'm amazed. It's as if sommat in Darren's animal instinct all of a sudden recognises that he can put his trust in Jim. But Jim says no.

'Fraid you're gonna have to stay here for a while,' he tells him. 'There's bleedin fuzz all over.'

'Right, Darren,' I says, once Jim has gone, 'we're gonna have us a tidy up.'

An we sets to work. We brushes an sweeps an dusts, then we mops an wipes where we can (though I'm reluctant to disturb too many of me things, so we just does round em) an by the time we've finished, the whole flat smells as sweet as a rose, I reckons.

Well, then we've worked up quite an appetite, so we has some toast an a drink, tho I'm already worryin about where the fuck I'm gonna get the money to buy more food once the few provisions I has in the cupboard has run out.

We've just finished when there's a knock at the door. It's loud, authoritative like, not like Jim's gentle scrabble at the door. Fuckin hell, I thinks to meself, tho I don't say nothin out loud, so's not to alarm Darren, I knows who this is. I spies through the hole, an sure enough, there's the constable what came the other day. He knocks again, nearly frightenin the bleedin wits outta me as I'm just standin on the other side.

'Quick,' I whispers to Darren, so low I doesn't know whether he hears me or not, 'you'll have to hide.'

An next thing, I'm pushin him into the bathroom, gettin him to climb up into the airin cupboard, with him only half realisin what's goin on. I covers him with the blanket, closes the door. Which clicks. Too loudly.

Christ, then I spots that there's still Darren's books out. I bundles them under the sink with a pile of newspapers on top. Then I slips back into the bathroom an flushes the toilet, then comes out closin the door behind me.

'Let us in, Glory,' the copper's shoutin from outside.

'Mrs Eden to you,' I mutters under me breath, but yells out irritably, 'All right, Officer, I'm comin.'

An I makes me way over an opens the door.

'Bleedin hell,' I says, 'a woman's allowed a crap in her own house, ain't she? What's all the bleedin fuss about?'

'Can we come in?' they asks, pushin their way past me.

Yeah, cos as usual it is a 'they'; the young policewoman from the other day's there too.

'If yer must,' I grumbles, followin them back into the room.

The constable sniffs the air, suspicious like, eyes the room.

'Smells nice in here, Glory. You been havin a clear out?'

'Yeah, Officer,' I says sarcastic like, 'Spring cleanin fever got to me a bit early.'

'Special occasion, is it?'

I shakes me head, shrugs.

'Expectin visitors, are we?' he says, real sly. 'Or maybe you got a visitor already? A little boy?'

'What the fuck d'yer take me for?' I says, aggressive like. 'I'm worried out me head about the whereabouts of that poor little boy, even came down the copshop to see if yer'd found him, I did, an if I understands yer correct, yer accusin me of havin him here. Blimey, never knew you fellas could be so fuckin ridiculous.'

But they both ignores me.

'Mind if we take a look round?' says the policewoman.

'What's the matter with you lot, ain't yer got nothin better to do, had a look the other day, din't yer? What d'yer think yer gonna find? Gold bleedin bullion or sommat? I can assure you I wouldn't be in this fuckin dump if I'd seen some of that.'

But they're already lookin, pokin round mongst piles of clothes an newspapers in the corner.

'Thought you'd looked in there already?' I says, bitter as fuckin almonds.

They carries on, an I can feel me heart thumpin in me chest like a great stick against the skin of a bass drum, makin the sides of me chest vibrate, makin me feel sick to the stomach. I feels the blood drainin from me face as they works their way towards the bathroom, the skin in me cheeks stretchin tight across me bones like parchment.

'What's the matter, Glory?' says the cop, 'You're lookin agitated.'

'Nothin,' I says. 'Just can't stand pigs snoutin around me front room what I've just cleaned.'

But I says it so quiet I don't think they hears me.

Thank Christ I didn't have no light in the bathroom. They opens the airin cupboard door, but it's so dim they don't see a thing, an luckily they ain't got their torches with em.

They comes back out into the front room, shruggin.

'Looks like you're clean, Mrs Eden,' says the constable, enjoyin the joke. 'For the time being.' Addin, 'But we may well be back...' Threatenin like.

'Any time, Officer,' I says, sarcastic as I can.

An they goes out, shuttin the door behind them.

I waits a bit, then checks the spy-hole, case they're standin there, listenin for clues, an I has me ears pricked up, alert as a fox, checkin for their footsteps along the corridor, the metallic clank of the lift door. Then, very soft like, I lets Darren out, me finger to me lips to warn him not to speak yet.

'See, Darren,' I says after a few minutes when I feels sure the bastards have gone, 'you'll have to go home sooner or later, me lad. They'll search until they finds you.'

'No,' he moans, his eyes fillin with tears, his bottom lip tremblin.

I makes a cup of tea an we sits down with Darren's books. I picks up *Jim's Day Out*. There's a picture of a little red-haired boy an a spaceship on the front, with some aliens pokin their heads out. Can't think it'll be of relevance to me, seein as the human kind seems alien enough as it is, let alone any such bodies from another planet, but I s'poses I has to start somewhere. I reads it to him slowly, makin the words out one letter at a time. I has a hard job of it. The words blur before me eyes, an if I gets too many before me at once they swirls like a shoal of letter-fishes in a whirlpool. Most words he knows to correct me; some he don't know himself. But slowly we gets the gist. An it ain't just that. It's the thrill of sittin there, tryin to work it out, workin it out together, feelin like we're makin progress. Wish I'd got that sort of pleasure when I was Darren's age. Might've made sommat of meself then, mightn't I? But life was fucked up all them years ago, what with Mum workin down the pub, an Him drinkin down the pub an me lyin in bed at home, petrified. Yeh, petrified I was. Not of ghosts an ghouls, nor snakes under the bed, nor burglars. Naa. It was the click of the door latch what got to me, His footsteps on the stairs.

I bin thinkin a lot about that recent like, this crazy old world of ours what we lives in. What a strange thing, this society where people goes to a place an exchanges money for a liquid that they keeps guzzlin back tho they ain't thirsty. The barmaid (in my case, me Mum) takes the cash an puts it in the till, then the landlord gives her some back, an she gives it to Him what gives it back to her behind the bar what gives it back to the landlord what gives some back to her what gives more liquid to Him to guzzle down. Cash an drink whizzin backwards an forwards, backwards an forwards across the bar an a gallon or two of piss goin down the fuckin lav. All in order for him to get smashed enough to go rollin home and pull the knickers off his ten year old daughter. Oh, an to line the landlord's pocket. See, the men wins all round, doesn't they?

I borrows one of Darren's pencils outta his pencil-case, finds a scrap of paper. An I makes a list of the words I ain't sure of. It takes me a long time to write them; me fingers feels stiff an ungainly like. I wants me letters to look neat an round like our Sis used to write, but it looks more like some spider got ink on the end of his little legs an walked around the page. Anyhow I'm in the middle of doin this, an actually, I has to admit, Darren's irritatin me, cos he's got bored with me slowness, an is holdin on to the kitchen door with his hands an swingin from side to side, swivellin on his heels. I'm tryin to concentrate an not be distracted an lose me rag, when Jim scrabbles at the door. I checks it's him an lets him in.

He's lookin pleased with himself. He's loaded down with several carrier bags an a rug rolled under his arm. Pink an cream, it is, just like one of those rolls of streaky bacon curled up an fastened with a cocktail stick an baked in the oven. Darren's stopped actin like Tarzan an is crowdin round Jim, helpin to unpack the bags. There's tins of paint, brushes, a packet of filler, a couple of cheap picture frames, an evenin paper an a bag of groceries for tonight.

'I'm invitin meself to dinner,' says Jim cheerfully. 'I think we deserves a little party.'

I'm glad to see a couple of bottles of booze amongst the groceries. I was beginning to wonder how the hell I was gonna get meself a drink that day, cos I knew I sure as hell couldn't go without one.

'How the bleedin heck you afford this lot anyway?' I asks Jim.

He looks at me all mysterious.

'Let's say someone owed me a favour.'

'I hope you ain't been doin nothin illegal,' I winks.

'Would I ever?' he says, pretendin to look affronted like. 'Now, let's get on with it.'

An he unwedges his overcoat an the jacket, lays them in a corner, rolls up his sleeves. It's amazin how wiry he is under all them layers. Yeah, sinewy. Must of bin strong as a fuckin ox once. What a fuckin waste.

'Jim,' I says, 'I can't do nothin without a drink.'

'Right, Glory,' he says, 'open up one of them bottles an we'll have a little refreshment while we work.'

I fetches two cups from the kitchen an pours out some cider. I doesn't offer none to Darren – there's enough with two old alkies in the house without a fuckin juvenile. When I've had a good sup, I joins the other two goin round fillin up holes in the plaster, all round the flat. There's cracks all over the place. Like great streaks of fork lightenin, they is, spreadin from ceilin towards the floor. There's holes too, big enough for rats to get through. Darren keeps teasin me, pretendin he's seen some little nose pokin out, or the streak of a tail disappearin behind the floorboards. Cos tho I doesn't mind em out in the street, it's another thing havin em in yer own home, ain't it?

By the time we've finished all that lot we're exhausted, we are. We leaves the filler to dry an Jim says we'll come back to the paintin another day. So we tucks into some bread an cheese an pickle an some tomatoes. Darren has lemonade an Jim an I finishes off the cider, opens a second bottle. We feels like kings, we does.

Afterwards we slumps on the settee, all three of us. Christ, I thinks to meself, we're like a regular little family, we are, huddled here together. As if Darren were me own boy, an Jim... bloody hell, I thinks, last week Jim was a fella what I passed in the park, some geezer to pass the time of day with, a geezer what did an didn't speak to yer, an if he chose not to, it made no difference to yer. An here he is, sittin on me settee, havin provided us with a stinkin great feed, laughin an jokin, makin Darren laugh, as if he'd been doin it all his bleedin life. It was as if that boy had cast some spell over him, there was such a bleedin change.

After a bit, Jim gets up, goes an fetches the newspaper from off the kitchen table, begins to read it.

'By Christ, Glory,' he says, 'seen this headline?'

'Don't be fuckin silly,' I says, irritable like, 'yer knows I can't make out a bleedin word. Don't tell me yer forget that already.'

But he ain't takin no notice. He's readin with Darren peepin over his shoulder.

'Lost boy may have been abducted, say police,' he's readin out.

'That ain't about who I thinks it is, is it?' I says.

Darren's grinnin.

'There's a photo of me in the paper,' he says.

'It ain't no laughin matter,' I says, serious like. 'Read the rest, Jim.'

It seemed like the cops were still searchin for Darren, but accordin to the paper, tho they had thought at first that he could of run away from the family home after an argument, it said that 'police were beginnin to fear that he may have been taken in by some element in the criminal community an had reason to be afraid for his safety.'

'Extensive dredgin of the canal and searchin of disused warehouses in the area have been carried out to no avail,' Jim read.

'Well well,' I says, smackin me lips complacent like, 'they didn't have a very good look round the station yard, did they? Otherwise they would of gathered the same clues as us.' I gives a big sigh, suddenly gloomy. 'But they'll keep pesterin us, won't they? Reckons you'll have to go back home sooner or later, me boy.'

'I ain't goin back,' Darren says, in a real grim little voice.

'Trouble is,' says Jim, 'you'll have to watch out they don't nab Glory for abduction.' An he turns to me, an adds, 'you could be put away for a long time, Glor, if they gets you on that.'

'I never abducted nobody,' I says, feelin real sullen like. 'Yer turned up here of yer own accord, didn't yer, Darren?'

'Course I did,' says Darren, concentratin on the drawin he's doin an not the conversation. Of which he is bored by then.

But Jim's solemn.

'Yer'll have to watch it, ' he says again, 'I reckons they could slam it on yer, easy as apple-pie.'

Fuckin hell, I mutters to meself. But then I shoves it to the back of me mind. An after a bit, Jim goes home, an Darren an I settles down for a bit of shut-eye.

Next day Jim's round early.

'Knock me down with a feather,' I says, openin the door to him.

'Jim's paintin an decoratin services,' Jim announces, grinnin that murky grin of his.

By Christ, I never seen him in such good form. He comes in an sets to work with the old paintbrush, even starts to whistle a tune in a low sorta raspy way. I makes a cuppa, an joins him, splish-splashin away with the old paintbrush to me heart's content. Darren finishes his cornflakes an comes an joins in too, tho he ends up gettin more on his shirt than he does on the fuckin walls. Still, we doesn't mind – we're all enjoyin ourselves, see.

Then the fumes starts to get a bit much an we has to open the frenchies. I've turned back to me wall when sommat catches the corner of me eye an I has the fright of me life. It's Darren. Leanin over the balcony railins, his legs danglin in mid-air. I opens me gob to shout at him to stand back down before he goes an bleedin plummets to his death, when I catches meself on. Cos, yer see, if one of them fuckin nosy neighbours sees or hears anythin what is goin on, we're up shit-creek, ain't we? I mean, since when did Ol' Glory have a kid stayin with her?

Anyhow, I says it real quiet. Come on in, Darren, you can't go out on the balcony in case yer seen. He's wobblin about, real precarious like, an I'm nearly havin a fuckin heart attack. At last he swings back down to safety, but when he turns round he ain't smilin that cheeky grin of his. His face his real grumpy. Trouble is, he's gettin bored, ain't he, can't stop fidgetin. He wants to get out of the flat, go play football with his mates. I tries to tell him his mates won't be there just now, they'll be at school, but it don't make him no happier.

'Yer can't go out,' I says, gettin exasperated like.

'I can do what I like,' he says, dead sullen.

'If yer goes out, the cops'll catch yer.'

'They never catched me before,' he says. Real cheeky.

I frowns but I don't say nothin. May be I should let him go. After all, what's it to me? Yet I'm scared what might fuckin happen to him, ain't I.

By afternoon the flat's beginnin to look real tickety-boo. I'm so pleased an grateful to Jim I wants to give him a big hug, but I just says ta an makes him a ketchup sandwich. Jim says, blimey is that all yer feedin the kid, an I says that's all I can afford, this ain't the fuckin Hilton. Then he follows me into the kitchen an says in a quiet voice so's Darren can't hear, I'll get sommat proper again for tonight. Bleedin heck, Jim, I whispers, where the bleedin hell yer gettin all the cash? Well, he looks right an proper embarrassed then. One all, I thinks.

'I got a trust fund, Glor,' he says, lookin at his feet. 'Ain't never told yer before, but there's quite a little sum put away for me. Just that I can't get at it all at once.'

'In that case, Jim,' I says, 'why the fuck yer livin like this?'

'Can't handle it, Glor,' he says.

'Please can I go out, Glory,' Darren pleads.

'I'll take yer out when it's dark,' I tells him. 'I promise.'

By the time the sky's bruisin purple, the front room is painted white all over an one coat of gloss is on too. Bathroom walls are painted too. Jim's been out an has bought some bits for a

nice stew what I has in the oven, an a bottle of whisky from
what I has a few nips while I'm cookin. Cookin. I ain't cooked
for fuckin years. Always makes do with a bit of bread an jam,
some cheese an biscuits maybe. Sometimes I scrambles meself
an egg. But this time, it's like I say, like havin a little family. So
I takes me time, browns the onion nice an slow, fries the meat,
takin care that it don't stick, chops the carrots nice an regular.

'Bloody hell,' I says to Jim as I'm rummagin through the
shoppin, 'you even bought herbs. Someone got you well trained.'

'Used to be a bleedin chef, din't I,' Jim rumbles into the door-
frame he's paintin.

'Christ,' I says, 'if I knewed that, you could of done the
bleedin cookin. It ain't gonna be no cord'n blue, yer know.'

He grins at me an carries on paintin. Bastard.

Anyhow, after I gets the stew in the oven, I knows I can't put
that other thing off any longer. Darren's asked to go out three
more times, an tho it ain't what I wants, I knows I has to face
it, an so I says to Darren there's time for me an him to go out
for our walk around the block. A tester, like. To see what we
can get away with.

It's like settin off a fuckin fire-cracker. He leaps up from where
he's been lollin around on the floor like a dog an rushes out the
door. As he does so, his sleeve brushes against the door-frame
an he gets paint all up it, but he don't care. He don't even care
about all the swear words that are comin out of Jim's mouth
like they was comin out the Channel Tunnel.

I'm shakin as we goes out into the corridor. What if a neighbour comes out his door an spots us? Hell, I thinks to meself,
what the fuck am I doin this for? I has enough trouble with me
nerves without this. Why doesn't I be done with it an hand the
little bugger in? I could pretend we're goin round the block an
end up goin past the copshop by mistake, I thinks. But then,
would they believe me when I said he'd turned up at me flat,
that I hadn't enticed him away from his rotten home? That's
what I wanted to know. Would they believe me? Cos that's the

trouble with what they calls the justice system. Yer guilty till yer proves yerself innocent. Despite what they says. Some fuckin justice.

We gets in the lift. Luckily there ain't no-one in it. An I'm prayin that there won't be no-one at the bottom neither. I has a swig of whisky from me flask, what I've topped up from Jim's bottle, while Darren's busy messin with the buttons in the lift.

'What's in there, Glory?' he says.

'Elixir, me boy,' I replies. 'Sommat for me sore throat.'

There I goes again, I thinks to meself. Helpin to build up a wall of untruths what makes up the reality of this child's world. That's what happens, ain't it? As we grows up, we comes to learn that there ain't a brick in that fuckin wall what ain't made of playdough, not a brick what ain't ready to disintegrate beneath the weather of adulthood. An then we struggles all the rest of our lives tryin to rebuild some kind of wall of our own, to make some fuckin sense of it all. An all the time we makes sure we're treatin the next generation just the bloody same.

When we gets outside I chooses the darkest way.

'Where d'you wanna go, Darren?' I asks.

But that too's a sham, cos I knows before he's even answered exactly where I'm gonna manipulate him to. An that's all the freedom he's gonna get.

He says he wants to go to the park. I says it's late, there'll be no-one about. He grumbles an I promises to take him the next day.

'But yer still won't be able to play with yer pals,' I tells him, 'less yer goes home first.'

'I'm not goin home,' he says. 'Any case, home is with you now, Auntie Glory.'

In no time at all we're back up the lift an shut safe an sound in the flat, where Jim's snoozin an boozin on the settee. I sighs with relief an helps meself to a well-earned tipple or two. Then I goes an tests the stew an the three of us settles down to a nice hot supper. I ain't eaten nothin so good in ages. An seein as no-one else seems to be so appreciative, I offers me own compliments to the chef. She bows an says, Madam, I'm honoured. At which Jim an Darren bursts out laughin. An we all drinks chin chin to the future, Darren with his lemonade an Jim an me with our tumblers of whisky.

Next day, as soon as we're up, Darren's naggin to go out. OK, OK, I says, tryin to think of some excuse for puttin the moment off, we've gotta wait for Jim.

'What'm I gonna do?' I whispers to Jim when he turns up. 'The kid's practically crawlin up the bleedin walls wantin to get out.'

Jim looks thoughtful. Then he says he's gotta go.

'Already?' I says, givin him a funny look, 'you only just bleedin got here.'

'Leave it to me,' he says, an goes out the door.

Which don't make it no easier, cos Darren's still naggin to go out.

We has to wait for Jim to come back, I tells him. But he's just bin, says Darren. Well, I says, gettin annoyed, Jim ain't got no key, an he's expectin to come back an find us in. So yer'll have to wait. To which Darren agrees, with a bit of a grudge.

But an hour goes by an Jim don't come. Two hours. An Darren's drivin me fuckin mad, he is. So, in the end, I gives in.

It's broad fuckin daylight an though he keeps the hood of his coat up, I knows that we're fuckin stupid. We walks around the park, says hello to the ducks, watches the squirrels, an fortunately we doesn't see none of his mates who might be scivin off school. Then we makes our way back towards our block, but Darren's naggin to buy some sweets, so I tells him to wait outside the newsagent's with his face to the shop window an on no account to move while I goes in an buys ten pence worth of chews. I'm just waitin to pay for them when I glances, anxious like, out on to the street. An me heart misses a beat. Cos there's two cops walkin right by. I've gone cold an I'm sweatin all at once, an I'm standin in that bleedin queue waitin to pay, thinkin keep cool, Glory, keep cool, but I'm so agitated I thinks I'm gonna die. I hands over me money, grabs me sweets an dashes outside.

There's no sign of Darren, nor them fuckin policemen. Bloody hell, I thinks, shakin like a twig in a force ten gale, that's the end of him. An I'm just feelin a flood of sobs comin over me what I doesn't want, not in the street, when the little bleeder jumps out from behind grabbin me on the fuckin shoulders, an shoutin, hey give me them sweets then! Bloody hell, I doesn't arf give him an earful.

Apparently, when he saw the cops comin along the road he hid behind some of those big wheelie bins. Yeah, he was a clever little kid all right. Nifty on his feet an all. But yer can imagine I couldn't get him back home fast enough. An I had the impression it'd even given him a bit of a fright, cos in the flat he acted quite subdued like.

So we sits quiet an tries to look at his books. An I has a go at writin me name, an by the afternoon I'm dead proud cos I can write it out without lookin at a copy. I can't wait for Jim to turn up so's I can tell him. Just like a little kid, I was.

It's well into the afternoon before Jim eventually appears. He's got his arm clenched across his chest like he's broke his fuckin arm. But it ain't that, he's got sommat hidden inside his coat. Calls over to Darren as soon as he's in the door.

'Brought you a playmate, Darren,' he rumbles, an from out of his breast he pulls a little pup, a snub-nosed thing with a little curly tail like a piglet, its coat a shiny smooth dark brown. It wriggles to the ground an goes chargin off round the flat. Darren's over the fuckin moon.

'Cor, thanks, Jim,' he says, chasin after the puppy, all the while grinnin from ear to ear.

The puppy goes an promptly has a widdle on the newspapers in the corner.

'Bleedin thing,' I laughs.

An Jim's standin there chucklin.

Anyhow the pup, what for some reason or other Darren decides to call Basher, does the trick. Darren shuts up about goin out for the rest of the day. We cautiously walks the puppy round the block after dark an there's no more talk about goin to the park.

Next mornin, tho, is a different kettle of fish altogether. Basher needs to go out to the park, Darren says. He don't need to, I argues, just play with him in the flat. Glory, Darren moans, he needs fresh air, somewhere to go to the toilet.

'Ain't my newspaper good enough for him?' I says.

'Glory, please let me take him to the park,' Darren pleads.

'Let's wait for Jim,' I says, usin the ruse of the day before.

But Jim don't turn up that day. An I spends the day livin on me nerves, wonderin how the hell I'm gonna keep this boy from goin out an gettin himself discovered. I distracts him with games, readin, playin with Basher, makin Basher a bed, makin Basher a lead by plaitin string… yeah, an any number of activities I could think of.

'I'll go out an buy Basher some food,' says Darren.

Me heart gives a leap, till I remembers Jim's left a few tins in a carrier in the kitchen.

'No need,' I grins in relief.

'When's Jim comin?' Darren asks just as the street lights are chargin up with their amber glow.

An I has to admit that I doesn't know.

'Spect he needed a rest from us today,' I says to Darren.

But all the same I'm as disappointed as he is.

When I wakes the next mornin the sun's shinin through the frenchies. So low in the sky it is, it's like a flippin light bulb in me eyes. I stretches an absorbs the warmth, content as a baskin cat. Cos it's bin a cold night an I've bin sleepin chilled. The flat seems strangely silent, an suddenly I has this horrible feelin

I'm alone. I jumps up quick as a fish jumpin in the river an goes to peep in the bedroom. Sure enough, Darren's bed's a tousle of clothes, an he ain't nowhere to be seen. Then I discovers a scrap of paper on the kitchen table with some writin on it. It's written in large simple letters, but I still takes a few minutes to figure it out. An when I does at last, a cold shiver snakes down me spine. *Gone out to play.* There ain't no sign of Basher. Guess he's gone an all.

Well, I'm resigned then. I puts the kettle on, potters about. What can I do now, I thinks. What's the sense in doin anythin? The cops'll pick him up, then it'll be back to that bastard brute of a father. They were only gonna get him sooner or later anyhow, weren't they? An this way at least I won't see no bother.

Then next thing I knows I've switched the kettle back off again, I'm gettin me bleedin coat an boots on an I'm settin off down the park to go an look for him. An course, he's there, ain't he, Saturday mornin like any other kid, playin football with his pals. Happy as Larry. With Basher chargin in amongst them, makin a nuisance of himself chasin the bleedin ball.

I watches them for a while, keepin out of sight like. An I thinks about leavin Darren be. But I knows the longer he stays the nearer he moves to gettin caught an that beatin that's bound to come from his Dad. So I plucks up courage an goes over. Maybe this is where he'll say bye-bye, Auntie Gloria, I don't need yer no more. His pals stare at me hard, wonderin who the fuck this old bag lady is, no doubt. While Darren grins at me. An carries on playin. Lookin as though he's tryin to impress.

Then I manages to catch him still for a moment an grabs him by the shoulder.

'Come on,' I says, 'yer'd better come home.'

He moans an groans, but he leashes Basher up an he comes. He knows he's put himself in danger. He knows his pals'll go home an say guess who I saw this mornin, an guess who he went away with.

I ain't cross with him. I knows it ain't much of a time he has up in that old flat of mine, even tho we has spruced it up. An I knows he knows that he shouldn't of gone to the park.

We walks back in silence. An all the time I'm thinkin to meself we're gonna have to go away, we can't stay in our little home no longer.

'What d'yer think about goin away somewhere?' I says to Darren.

He shrugs. 'It'd be all right. Why?'

'Trouble is, Darren,' I says, 'if we stays here, the police're gonna find yer pretty damn quick.'

He nods, his little face pale. The whole thing has got too big for him to handle.

'I tell yer what,' I says, as we steps into the lift, 'shall I just take yer home to yer Mum?'

But he shouts a real violent 'No', an starts to blubber.

It's more than I can fuckin chew, I can tell yer. All I wants to do is stay in this nice fresh-painted flat an try to make sommat more of me life than what I've made of it up till now. I was even thinkin of goin down the centre an gettin lessons, learnin to read an write proper like.

I makes some tea when we gets in, a weak one for Darren, an mine with a dribble of whisky what's left in the bottle. I wishes Jim'd turn up, but there ain't no sign, an I can't go lookin for him cos I can't trust Darren not to disappear off again. Besides, I knows we ain't got no time before the police're gonna be here.

I gives Darren some biscuits to dunk in his tea, an I nibbles at one or two while I'm packin up a bag. I gets Darren to collect his things too, but he's slow an I ends up doin most of it meself. But I'm worried. Cos although I'm packin, I doesn't know where we're goin an in any case, I'm short on the readies. An I'm wonderin how the hell we're gonna manage.

'We'll have to go, whatever,' I says to Darren.

'Yep,' he says. Just like that. He knows we ain't got no choice.

We're ready an we're just peepin out the spy-hole to check the coast is clear when I hears someone walkin along the corridor.

It's Jim. I opens the door, lets him in, an before he has a chance to get a word in edgeways I tells him what's happened an what we're up to.

When I thinks back, I remembers how rough he was lookin, but at the time I doesn't ask him how he is, an he don't say. Instead he's rummagin in his pocket an shovin some notes into me hand, more notes than I've ever held before in me hand at one time, an wishin us good luck. Send us a postcard, he's chucklin. But his face don't say that. It says, Christ I'm gonna miss you.

An I can't handle that at all.

'Christ, Jim,' I says, starin down through tears at the money in me hand, 'can yer spare us all this?'

'Yer just take it, Glory,' he says.

An I ain't got time for more questions cos he's shovellin us out the door, helpin me to tuck Basher up inside the breast of me coat, tellin us to hurry, tellin us to go down the stairs while he goes down the lift just in case there's anyone official like needs distractin, tellin us to go the back way round to the coach station, that there's buses settin off up north every hour.

An cos I hadn't thought what we was gonna do, we just does as he says, an in no time at all, we're pullin outta the coach station in one of them dirty great flash coaches, headed for the motorway an the north. An I'm lookin back at the Ford garage, our block of flats standin grey against a grey sky, the black mirror windows of the police station, the old pillars of the courts, an I thinks this is the only place what's bin my world before. An it feels a bit like I'm bout to drive off the edge, it all seems so strange, me an this little boy beside me firin headlong together into the future.

Next thing I knows we're whizzin up the motorway. Darren's fallen asleep, his little brown head laid against me arm. Even Basher's stopped drivin me mad with his wrigglin inside me coat, an has settled down to a twitchin puppy sleep. What the fuck are yer doin, Glory, I asks meself, as I studies Darren's pale cheeks, smooth as waxed cheese, the dark brows, usually

puckered, lookin as if they've been ironed. Such peace just
now. Such peace.

I gazes out the window. There's fields stretchin to the horizon,
striped with roads an hedges, splatted with buildins, like someone's got a paintbrush an dipped it in a giant can of buildin paint
an flicked it across the countryside, like Darren when he was
helpin me an Jim paint the flat. But overall the impression is of
green. I never seen it before, so much green. I can't believe it.
It's like this coach is a great washin machine, an it's washin all
the dirt an grey an grime outta me eyes, replacin it with green.
With sheep an cows an barns full of hay. An trees. Lumpin great
trees with their bare spreadin branches networkin the sky. But
then yer stares close an yer sees all the other traffic roarin up
alongside yer, an yer feels like yer part of a great flow of dirt
spillin from one city to another, leavin yer grime behind en route.
An it makes me feel guilty. Like a criminal.

Then I sets to wonderin where the hell all these folks is goin.
After all, I thinks, they ain't all rushin away with a little boy
what's afraid of his parents. So what the fuck're they doin?
Fascinated, I am. I sets to try to get glimpses of faces in cars,
tryin to sus out what they're doin an who they are. There's
business people an workmen, women with babies, groups of
young lads in cars what looks like they're about to fall to bits.
The cars that is, not the lads, ha ha. Though I dares say the
lads're probably fallin to bits too, in a manner of speaking. Cos
there's not many what has a life that's whole these days, is
there? Naa, their lives're in bits. Splintered through they are,
with pain an discomfort an hardship. Just like me an Darren.

Suddenly I shivers, disturbin Darren, who opens his eyes,
looks around as if he can't quite believe where he is, who he's
with, then leans back again snugglin into me. I'm shiverin cos
this thought has suddenly occurred to me, see. I'm wonderin if
me an Darren are what yer'd call fugitives. Are we gonna be
runnin away for the rest of our lives, I'm askin meself. That
case, we're gonna have to make plans. When we gets off this

coach, we're gonna be facin a whole new world. Should we, I wonders, give ourselves new names? Change our looks?

It's already gettin dark by the time we arrives, an I knows it won't be long before the shops close. So we puts Basher on the leash an heads straight towards what looks like the centre of town. I doesn't want to ask no-one the way, draw attention to ourselves like, so we has to follow our noses. I uses a bit of Jim's money to buy us a sandwich an a drink cos we're pretty peckish by then, an we munches into the sandwiches while we looks for a charity shop. Comes across one of them, an after a few minutes in there dashes off to a chemist's. We just bout gets what we wants from there before the security geezer comes along an boots us out.

'Closin time, I'm afraid, Madam,' he says, lookin down his nose at me an Darren.

All the same, I don't think I bin called 'Madam' before. We struts out the shop like we was Lord an Lady Muck.

Next thing, we finds a Ladies, locks ourselves, pup an all, in the mother an baby room. I makes Darren dip his head in the sink while I applies the dye I bought, rubs his hair dry with paper towels, combs it out. He complains like mad at first an cries when he gets some of the bleedin stuff in his eyes, an even more when I splashes cold water into his face to wash it out, but I tells him it's all for the best. It's like playin detectives, I says. An that shuts him up. Then he stares into the mirror, a look of wonderment upon his face, while I paints freckles on his creamy cheeks, a few on his little snub nose.

'This is what it must be like behind the scenes at the bleedin theatre,' I says to the fair-haired little stranger what's starin back at me, forgettin me language.

When I've finished, he giggles an parades around in a circle, struttin his head like a bleedin cockbird. Then I washes me own hair, dyes that too. Only black. Gets in a bit of a mess with dye drippin down me neck, cos me hair's that long it ain't easy to manage. An by then there's someone rattlin the door handle. Then they starts knockin, askin if we're gonna be long. But I doesn't want to be hurried. So I just doesn't reply. I dries meself off as best I can, then puts on a bit of make-up. By then we can hear a baby beginnin to cry outside. I doesn't like to hear it, like I told yer before, but I'm determined to finish the transformation, as it were. There's more knockin at the door. An the baby's howlin louder.

'Bloody rude buggers,' I says to Darren.

Next I changes me coat for the one I got from the charity shop, dumps the other in the bin. Makes me heart bleed, that does. Never could bare throwin nothin away, specially a perfectly good coat like that one, what I has become attached to. Still, I thinks, that's the price you gotta pay, ain't it, an remembers what Basher did all down it on that fuckin coach journey.

We has a bit of a shock when we eventually comes out the mother an baby room. The woman's standin there with her baby yowlin its little head off, an next to her is a real hostile lookin attendant. In her hands she's got her keys poised, ready to let herself in on us like. When she sees us she starts mouthin off about the facilities bein for mothers an babies only an all that, but catchin up Basher into me arms as best I can with all the other bags, we scarpers while she's in full flow, charges away off down the street.

'Now,' I says smilin breathlessly at Darren once we got far enough away to slow down, 'we're two different people, ain't we, from what we was. P'raps we'd better have two different names. What d'you think?'

'Michael,' says Darren. 'I'll be Michael. He's me best mate back home.'

'OK,' I says, 'what about me?'

'Oh, you'll always be Glory,' he says, smilin up at me.

We manages to find a cheap boardin house. It ain't exactly salubrious like, but it'll do for one night. They takes dogs, an I has the feelin that there they won't ask no questions neither. Which they doesn't. We books in as Mrs Gardener an grandson, Michael. I got Gardener from 'Eden', which, if you remembers, is me real surname. Gardener... Eden... get it?

Well, to us, it's luxury whatever it may be to folks what is used to hotels an that. We sleeps like bleedin tops we does, gets up for the cooked breakfast an is on the road again by ten. Yeah, cos that's what we are. On the road. I was chewin it over before I went to sleep, an I couldn't stop worryin. Wherever we goes, I'm thinkin, we're bound to attract attention, whatever the colour of our hair, whatever we calls ourselves. We can't stay in this city, I tells meself. What we needs is a place away, hidden from peerin eyes. So we heads back for the bus station, decides to take a bus to the moors. Darren does most of the sortin out. Reads the timetable, he does, spots the number on the front of the bus. Such a quick little lad, an so grown up for his age. I tells ya, I would of bin fuckin lost without him.

At first the countryside is quite flat, like a vast plain. When yer looked round yer could see the city behind yer for ages. Then the bus started to climb up into these little villages. Up an down. Up an down. Beautiful it is. Only, Darren an me is feelin sick.

'Bloody hell,' I says to Darren, 'when we gonna get off?'

But he says we can't till we get to the moors. The moors is where we paid for an we has to keep goin. Course, I knows he's right.

At last we gets out at this village what seems to be the end of the line. Darren says there's a notice, says it's the Gateway to the Moors. That'll do, I says.

It's a pretty place, a lot of real old buildins an that, built of wonky grey stone with ivy crawlin up the sides, cottages that looks as though they're about to go scrumblin to the ground. That's another of me words I made up. Scrumblin.

The village is bustlin with folks doin their shoppin an that. Tryin to behave like any other tourist, we buys ourselves a pie an a bar of chocolate each, case we needs some energy later. Then

we sets off up the road. We can't stay there, I says to Darren.
We has to get right away, find somewhere inconspicuous like.

'Bet you can't spell that,' says Darren. 'Inconspicuous.'

Bet I can't neither, I says.

It had bin rainin earlier, but now the sky had brightened, an
it looked like the whole countryside had bin varnished. I never
realised there was so many different shades of brown. Even the
mud at the edge of the road was the richest chocolate you could
ever imagine. An it all blended in with the greens an olives of
the fields, an mossed-up trees, ivy, an the rusty orange of fallen
leaves on the woodland floor. Then there was the bluey-green
fir trees, too.

'Look,' I squeals to Darren, 'a rabbit.'

Basher's standin watchin it, blinkin shyly. He ain't developed
the killer instinct. Not yet, any rate. We stands watchin the rabbit
as it scampers off, the white patch of its tail bobbin up an down.

'Grandma says they're vermin,' Darren says. 'Granddad always
used to shoot em.'

'Poor little buggers,' I replies.

Then, real sudden like, out of the hedge that lines the road
on one side appears a large bird. It's wonderful, it is, flecked in
browns an white on its body, while its head is red with a shining
green-blue neck an a ring of white round it like a collar – real
exotic like. Darren says it's a pheasant an they shoots them too.
Well, I ain't never seen a pheasant before, an I sure as hell wouldn't
shoot such beauty. That's all men seem to do, ain't it, I thinks
to meself, destroy things what are beautiful.

However, I shoves unpleasant thoughts away, an breathes in
the scented air. An for a few moments I feels like I'm in heaven.

It don't last though. Cos it's cold, an Darren's complainin
about his achin legs already, says his toes are frozen. It ain't
surprisin really. He's only got thin socks on, an there's a split in
one of his trainers. Whereas me, for one I'm used to trampin
about the place, an second, I got me trusty old boots on, ain't I,
an socks on top of me tights.

Anyhow, I goads Darren on, says there'll be somewhere to shelter in a while. We breaks into one of the bars of chocolate, an goes chompin up the road. A great black bird is perched on top of the hedge, a rook or a crow or some such item, its huge wings black an glossy an grooved like a gramophone record, sittin there all majestic like till the last minute when we're almost up to it, an it flaps its great wings an flies off across the field.

'This is better than the fuckin zoo,' I says to Darren.

He grins, but I can tell that he's losin his sense of humour, poor little chap.

Then, almost as much of a surprise as that fuckin pheasant, we comes to the end of the woodland an we're standin lookin down on the most beautiful stretch of moorland yer could ever wish for. Rollin on like unbroken waves, lappin over each other for miles an miles an miles. Yeah, lappin as far as the eye could see, those moors was. All in browns an rusts an a dull sort of purply colour. There's farms dotted here an there, too, buildins clustered together like little models, an I can hear the occasional bleatin of sheep, from far below. They looks so small, they're just like little cream pebbles dotted around the fields. An apart from the sheep it's silent. It's so bleedin silent, I can almost hear the thoughts grindin in me head.

I don't know whether it's cos of the beauty of it all, or the strain of the journey an uncertainty bout the future an whatnot, but I starts to blubber. Which don't help Darren none, cos he starts to blubber too.

'Ain't nature better than people,' I sobs.

An he comes close to me an pats me hand with his, like he was the adult an I was the child.

At last I blows me nose an we manages to find a bench in a sort of car park place, an we sits there an eats our pie, an listens to the silence. Then we sets off again, carryin the pup this time, cos the poor little blighter's worn out, he is. Off down the hill. Like goin into the wilderness, it was.

I'm serious by then about lookin for a shelter, even beginnin to panic a bit, cos we're losin the light, an I wishes Jim had come with us, cos surely he would know what to do. We've lost the hedges an the fields now, an most of the woodland, an the road's skirted by ferns spreadin like rust across the moors (Darren says it's bracken, cos he's seen it before when he's bin visitin his Grandma). But there ain't much else. There's some funny stone wall things, built in a line across the moors, what Darren says are for these lords an that that goes shootin, but they ain't got no roofs, which ain't much good in the pourin bleedin rain now, is it? A grey-yella light is strainin down between the clouds, withered windswept trees stand out black against it. An I realises then the meanin of the word 'bleak'. The wind's got up an is whippin around us, cold, unforgivin, an I begins to feel real frightened. Real frightened.

It's then that I notices a track veerin off down towards one of the valleys where I can see a fair number of buildins scattered about.

'We'll go down there, Darren,' I says. 'Get outta the wind a bit. Besides, I bet there's a barn or sommat we can shelter in.'

We trundles down there. It's a bit muddy, an Darren's complainin that his feet're wet.

'Not far now,' I says.

But in reality how the fuck would I know how bleedin far it is?

We're cuttin down through a patch of pine forest. The light's turned more orange by then, the last throes of the day. I has me eyes on the forest floor, watchin where I steps, in case I trips. It's a layer of orange needles. Like God has gone an dropped his toolbox an hundreds of tiny rusty nails have spilled all over the ground. An there's small pine cones too, like pale grey-brown wooden flowers, perfect in shape. Every so often there's an enormous mound covered in the same fox-red needles, what Darren says're ant-hills. In the distance a sheep bleats.

I stops a minute, reaches into me pocket an takes out me flask, has a swig. It's the first proper drink I've had all day. I'm worried though. I ain't got a lot left.

About halfway down from the top of the moor to the bottom
we comes across these old farm buildins, all dilapidated like.
There's stones sprawled across the field where it stands, like peas
spilled across a table from a spoon. There ain't no roof on the
farmhouse itself, but one of the outbuildins looks like sommat
more of a shelter, so we steps into that. We has the fright of our
lives as three or four sheep comes chargin out of the darkness
an goes gallopin past us down the field. Guess we gave them a
pretty good scare an all.

At first we can't make out much at all, it's so dark, an we
ain't got no torch. Just a few matches left in the box what I'm
savin to light me last two ciggies. However, after a few moments
we begins to be able to make things out, an fumbles around in
the gloom gatherin bits of twig an stuff to make ourselves a bit
of a fire in what looks like an old fireplace at one end. I adds a
few bits of rubbish out of me pocket an at last we thinks we got
enough an I sets a match to it. Curses cos the first two matches
gets blown out with the draught. But then it seems to catch an
soon we has a blaze goin what cheers us up no end. Then we
sits an eats all the rest of the chocolate an a couple of stalish
rolls what I discovers is left in the bottom of me bag.

By this time Darren's in a lot better humour, an we makes
jokes about the boy scouts an whatnot, says we're gonna have
a parley an a dib dib dib round the fire. Only thing is, we're
thirsty, but that'll have to wait till mornin, I says, cos we doesn't
know where there's water an we ain't goin nowhere to look for
it, cos it's bleedin pitch outside. We finds some old sacks in the
corner, makes a bed of sorts, an huddles down together as best
we can. I'm regrettin throwin that old coat of mine away by then,
it would of made a fine blanket. Stead, we shivers the night
away, Darren sleepin more than me, I thinks, cos I can't get
used to the quiet. There is sounds, but they're different from
the roar of traffic. The low whistle of the wind threadin its way
in an out of the buildins, a sheep bleatin, a high-pitched screech
what I thinks might be an owl but sends shivers down me spine

anyway. An I thinks about Darren, an the responsibility of havin him, an hopes I doesn't crumble beneath the weight of what I've taken on.

SIS

Gerald said my face was a picture when I discovered that photo of her in the paper. Fancy that, my kid sister, little Gloria, ending up as a child abductor. Perhaps it was because she never had the chance to have any of her own. Never really settled down, though I've learned since that she was married for a few months. But apparently that didn't work out. Then there was all that stuff with our Dad. Well, I never think about it really. It's something I push away if it ever comes into my mind. But then it wasn't me he bothered with really. It was her. Sometimes I wonder if she goaded him on. Knowing what I know now, about her madness and that, I think it might have been her inviting him, her with her crazy ideas, though at the time I was sympathetic. Naturally. Gerald says he wonders if she was making it all up, that it never happened at all. Perhaps he's right. After all, Mum never seemed to know anything about it. And surely she would have done. Don't you think?

GLORIA

In the mornin the wind's changed direction an there's a brilliant blue sky. The sun's sparklin down on the frost like a bleedin toothpaste advert, an once again I'm astounded by the beauty of the place. But we can't stick around gawpin cos there's no water here, it seems, an we're gaspin of thirst. So we gathers our things an sets off down the valley hopin that there'll be water down further an also a shop somewhere where we can buy some breakfast.

We makes our way along the track, the ground hard as fuckin pavements. Then it starts to get overgrown, an we has a bit of a battle through broken brown ferns what seems set like traps to trip yer up, an further on, tall reeds, where the ground is all soggy despite the frost, an we're gettin our feet wet an muddy again. Or should I say wetter. Cos our shoes (especially Darren's) ain't really dried off overnight tho we put em near the fire. There's trees down there too. Looks real old, they does, all bent an gnarled, like old men standin with their arms adrift. I wishes that I knew all the names of all the different species of tree, so's I could tell em to Darren. If Jim was here, I says to meself, he would know their names.

Darren's way ahead of me anyhow, an he's shoutin cos he's found a spring. I can hear it bubblin away before I sees it. I catches up with him an stands for a minute starin at the water tumblin down over the rocks an through the reeds. Then we stoops down an drinks from it. I ain't ever tasted water so sweet. An I marvels at the things what're on this planet, an thinks what the bleedin heck is people up to makin up all these concoctions with all those bleedin chemicals when we've got sommat so pure an, I think the word is, quaffable. But it ain't altogether good for me, cos it's too late, ain't it? I *has* to have the bleedin chemicals.

Anyhow, all three of us has a good drink an continues on

down the track. We ain't gone very far when we turns a corner an comes across an old cottage what's all boarded up an that. There's a great crack zigzaggin down one of the outside walls, from the chimney to the ground, looks like it's gonna split the house in two. The garden's all overgrown, the gate's wedged tight with mud an weeds. Cos of course we can't resist goin in to have a look. We checks to make sure there ain't no-one about first, no farmer or nothin, then we tries the front door, an it opens with a grindin against the tiles inside where it's swollen.

It's dark an musty an we moves around gingerly like.

'What if someone lives here?' Darren says, real nervous.

'Oh, no-one don't live here,' I says. 'There ain't been nobody here for years, I wouldn't think. Cept somebody's bleedin chickens,' I adds, as me eyes gets used to the dark an I sees all this shit an feathers caked to the floor. 'An it looks like even they moved out.'

But there's a kitchen sink with a tap, cupboards, fireplaces in every room, an old toilet an bath upstairs.

'Fit for kings, me boy,' I says to Darren.

'We gonna stay here, then?' Darren asks.

'Darren,' I says, 'I think you an me found a home.'

I bends down, fumbles beneath the sink, lookin for a stop-cock. Sure enough I finds one and turns it on. Tells Darren to try one of the taps. A flow of water splutters out.

'Eureka!' I says.

'I'm hungry,' says Darren.

'I'll tell yer what,' I says, 'you stay here an see if yer can gather some twigs an stuff for a fire, an I'll go an do a bit of a recky.'

Further along the track I comes to a farm what is obviously inhabited. I sneaks by hopin no-one'll see me. The track's open by then, lookin out on one side over a patchwork of fields of sheep an cows, an stretchin up to moorland on the other side where more sheep're grazin. I arrives at the end of the track what comes out onto a loop of road windin down to the very bottom of the valley an up the other side. There ain't exactly a bleedin supermarket. Fact, I can't see nothin but the occasional grey stone house an a lot of countryside. Under different circumstances like, I thinks I could sit an paint it. Like a lost valley, it is, all quiet but for the sound of a distant tractor, an the animals buttin in with a baa here an a moo there. That starts me off hummin Old MacDonald, an I hums it all the way back to the cottage.

I finds Darren full of glee. He's already managed to pile up a stack of twigs outside the back door. He's arranged them roughly in the shape of a man, put a load of ivy on the top for the hair. Then he shows me another stick what he says is his gun, puts it to his shoulder an pretends to shoot, makin a raspin noise with his mouth.

'I'm shootin me Dad,' he says, grinnin from ear to ear.

But it gives me a turn, it does. Cos I knows in a way he means it, on account of the thoughts I've had meself about Him. I doesn't like it. An it don't give no answers. Bein violent, I mean.

'Don't do that,' I says, but he don't stop till I suggests we lights a fire.

An that's a disaster to begin with. Whole room fills with billowin, it does. Think there must of been not just one bird's nest up the chimney but a whole flamin city of em. Coughin an splutterin, I pokes up there with Darren's stick-gun, an after a load of twigs an stuff's fallen down, very nearly puttin the whole fuckin fire out, it begins to draw. That gives us a bit of light as well as warmth.

'I'm gonna have to go back to the village,' I announces. 'There ain't no shops round here, an I'm gettin bleedin hungry even if you ain't. Yer can play round here while I'm gone.'

But he ain't havin none of it. He don't want to stay there on his own. Yer'll get tired with all the walkin, I says. Won't, he says. Yer can't go, I says, what if someone was to see yer. In disguise, ain't I, he says. He stands there, all stubborn, his little

fists clenched at his sides. No, I says. He says, there ain't nothin
yer can do to stop me. Listen to me, young chap, I says, yer'll
do as I asks, an no nonsense.

Well! He stamps his feet an howls, tells me I doesn't care
about him an all sorts of rubbish, an I stands there all perplexed
like. Then I says, right me boy, I'm takin yer home. He stops
immediately, stares at me cold. That's right, I says, I'm takin
yer back to yer Dad. Then he goes all quiet, disappears upstairs
an sulks in one of the bedrooms. An when I'm settin off all I
can get out of him is a grunt when I asks him if he'll be all right
while I'm gone, an another grunt when I says are yer sure.

'An don't speak to nobody,' I calls as I'm goin back down
them stairs. 'In fact, don't let no-one even see yer. An that goes
for Basher an all.'

An Basher looks up at me with his pleadin doggy eyes, an the
pair of them has made me feel like I'm some tyrant, not fuckin
tryin to do me best to look after them.

An off I goes, trampin back up that fuckin track. I calms
down after a bit, sets to thinkin that if sketch pads an pencils're
cheap an I've got enough money, I might buy one, see if I can't
sit an draw some of this lovely country, seein as I'm gonna
have time on me hands. Then I starts worryin about money.
After all, what Jim gave me weren't a bottomless pit, an I wonders what the fuckin hell we're gonna do after it runs out.

It takes about an hour an a half to reach the village, walkin
at a quickish pace, like. By which time that tum of mine's goin
fuckin frantic. I wanders round the minimarket, chatterin to
meself. Tellin meself that I has to take care buyin things, that
I've gotta get things what'll last, an things that ain't too heavy.
I buys nosh for the day but also packet soups, instant whip,
powdered milk. It takes me ages cos I can't read the packets
too well. An also I has to watch that it ain't gonna come to too
much. In the end I goes to the check-out an takes a chance.

'Visiting are you?' says the check-out girl, real friendly like. But
I ain't used to people speakin to me, an it makes me freeze inside.

'Yeah,' I mumbles, tryin to muster a smile. 'Holiday.'

She tells me how much I owes her an I starts to try to count out me money. I can feel the woman behind me starin at me. Fuck, I thinks, it's the last bleedin thing I wants. Attention. Might as well hand Darren in to the fuckin police right away in that case. I shoves a couple of notes at the check-out girl.

'Been here before, have you?' she says, takin the notes an smilin as she hands me the change. 'Only, your face is familiar.'

'No,' I says. 'Never.'

'Well, enjoy your stay,' she says.

Thanks, I mutters, an skedaddles outta the shop. Then I remembers I wants to buy a postcard to send to Jim, so I goes back in again, passin the other woman on her way out, who gives me another funny look. The girl's not at the check-out, she's talkin with a geezer in a suit what looks like the manager. Whisperin sommat with a frown on her face. She glances down towards the till, an when she sees me she says sommat else to the bloke an comes down, blushin, as if she's embarrassed to see me. I pays for me postcard an goes out. Feelin fuckin unsettled, I can tell yer. So unsettled I opens the whisky I've bought an has a swig, cos it's more than me nerves can cope with. It's then that I notices a newspaper folded up in a rack hangin from the wall, with Darren's face peerin out at me from the front page, an what's worse, one of me an all. Where the bleedin heck did they get a photo of me from, I thinks. Then I remembers the police records.

I scarpers back up the road, munchin biscuits an the crust off the end of the bread as I heads back towards the cottage. At a fair lick, I can tell yer. All I wants is to get back, make sure Darren's safe.

Weather's changed again. Ice has melted an it's gone real gloomy like. By the time I'm to the moors I feels drizzle on me face. If yer looked in one direction along what Darren told me was the scarpment, it was still quite clear, just a wisp or two of mist risin up from the valley bottom. It was as if God was lyin down there, enjoyin himself by the river, sprawled out with his hands beneath his head, elbows splayed, smokin a cigar. But when yer looked in the other direction towards the great wedge of rock what pokes out on to the moor, well yer couldn't see nothin, just great billowin clouds what looked like the grey smoke that billowed out of the cottage chimney earlier, as if He'd set light to the whole bleedin lot. Clouds rollin up the scarpment, as if they was bein sucked up from bottom to the top, then suddenly let go, allowed to roll right back down again. An I can't believe it's the same bleedin place as earlier. An I feels like me spirits are swirlin in with them clouds, an they doesn't know in what direction to roll.

On the way down the hill I notices a tree trunk where the top's snapped off in the wind. Standin there all jagged, it is, just like a match that you snaps in half with yer finger an thumb. Only bigger, of course. An stuck in the clench of the splinters, I notices someone has put the top half of a smashed bottle all green an jagged, just like the tree trunk, only stuck the other way up, an, course, the two items are a different green entirely. One a soft brownish green, speckled, the other a strong loud green, stark an plain. It's like the meetin of the two jagged edges of man an nature, I thinks. Then I hears Jim's voice in me head, sayin, steady on, Glor, you ain't bleedin Aristotle, gal. An I walks on, turnin me thoughts to domestic matters, such as food an the fact that we've run out of clean clothes an all that sorta stuff what never much bothered me before Darren come along.

Even before I enters the cottage I senses sommat. The front door's wedged open, an when I gets inside, I sees the fire's almost burnt out. This ain't right, I thinks. Grump or not, Darren is much too keen on fires to let it out. Sommat must of happened for him not to tend it. Panic sets in. I rushes from room to room callin his name. But there's no answer. I'm fuckin furious with meself for leavin him in that sulk. Supposin he's run away? Supposin he's followed me to the village an got lost? Worse than that, what if they've bin for him already? An icy wave of fear engulfs me. They've took him away, I sobs to meself. I charges outside, scours the ground for prints of their heavy boots in the mud. An then I hears sommat. Voices. Children's voices, what sounds like they're down by the river.

I heads off down through the trees, quiet but quick as I can, following the sound of them till I can see Darren sittin in a circle with three other kids playin some sorta game. I doesn't know whether to be relieved at findin him or angry that he's allowed himself to be discovered. I hesitates. Then I goes over. Darren looks up at me all matter of fact.

'This is Glory,' he announces to the other kids.

One of em offers me an apple from a bag. I stands there for a minute, tryin to keep me cool. Ta, I manages to say at last, an reaches out to take it. I'm hungry, but I'm too upset to eat so I shoves it into me pocket.

'An where yer from?' I asks, keepin me voice even.

From the farm, they says.

'Oh really?' I says, nice an polite. But I ain't feelin nice an polite inside. I'm still ragin.

'Better come home now,' I says.

An, grumblin, he follows me up the hill, Basher chargin on ahead.

'Bloody hell, Darren,' I says, once we're inside the safety of the cottage, 'you tryin to get us into trouble?'

He looks up at me, tears fillin his eyes.

'I was just makin friends, Glory,' he says.

An I knows I can't be angry no more.

'Yeah,' I says, gentle, an tousles his hair with me hand. 'You was.'

An sets about rekindlin the fire.

Then we unpacks the goodies an helps ourselves to chunks of bread with corned beef an a fresh tomato each. Plates is a bit of a problem, but I'd bought some plastic cups, so's we can drink water with our meal, mine with a little drop of whisky in it. An that, I can tell yer, warmed the cockles of me heart.

After, Darren sits down to help me write the postcard to Jim. It takes forever to get the words down, an there's so much I wants to say, I doesn't know what to put in an what to leave out. But eventually I gets sommat down an I feels real proud. Me very first postcard. Next, I says to Darren, I'll be writin a fuckin book. Then we discovers that I doesn't even know the proper address, an we ends up puttin a bleedin description of the whereabouts of his flat on the card, as if we was the fuckin AA tellin the postman how to get there. Then we gets fits of the giggles, an everything seems all right again, as if we're gonna stay like that for ever.

It's already late afternoon an I'm afraid of losin the daylight, so I sets about havin a rummage round the place. There's some old blankets in what looks like the airin cupboard, so I gets them out. Meantime I've sent Darren rummagin outside. He comes back with all sorts, he does. Long straight sticks what we ties together with string from the trusty ball I keeps in me bag. Darren's stick-gun goes in the middle (much to his annoyance, but he sees the funny side of it after a while) and that makes a kind of broom, so's we can sweep all the rooms out. We doesn't have a dustpan so we just sweeps the mess into a corner of each room outta the way. I really doesn't know what's got into me, I never bin so domesticated like since havin this boy in me care. Is this what motherhood does to yer, I wonders, makes yer want to build little nests all the time?

By this time, it's dark. We makes our beds up in the sittin room on account of havin the fire in there an it bein warmer. We has blankets an old bracken stalks an fir branches for mattresses what Darren has collected. I thinks it looks prickly sort of beddin, but I don't say nothin. Then I mixes up some packet soup, guessin more than readin the instructions cos it's too dark for me an Darren to make it out, an we ain't quite got our lightin system sorted out. Still, we slurps it up, then settles into bed.

SIS

Sending that postcard to that friend of hers (Jim, was it?) was the silliest thing. But that was what she was like. She didn't have half the common sense that most of us have. Not that it makes any difference to me, you understand. After all, she had what was coming to her, didn't she? You don't just abduct a little boy like that and think you can get away with it now, do you? Even if you believed her story about that dad of his beating him, it was a damn silly thing to do, because you can't take the law into your own hands, can you? She would never have made a detective, showing herself in the village like that. I mean, she wasn't exactly inconspicuous, her with her wild grey hair flowing about her shoulders – well, black, if she'd dyed it, as she says – like some old hag, and those black teeth. Besides, she must have stunk to high heaven. She was never the best of people when it came to personal hygiene, but from what I can gather, she went round in a cloud of her own aroma. Well, you can't help but notice someone like that. Then she went and allowed him to mix with those kids. I would have kept my head right down if that had been me. I wouldn't even have lit a fire. After all, it was bound to raise suspicion, chimney smoke rising from a cottage that hadn't been lived in for years. Like I say, she would never have made a private detective.

GLORIA

Next day we has an early mornin call. It's the kids wantin Darren to play. They've brought us taters an some fresh milk in a jug. We has some on our cornflakes. Eats out of two old Pot Noodle tubs what the kids've brought. An Basher gets a slurp or two out of yesterday's corned beef tin. Straight from the cow, they says the milk is. All rich an creamy.

Yeah, we chomps while the kids stands around gawpin. I says to Darren afterwards that I don't reckon they seen no city slickers like us before, that's why they stares so much. An we has a good laugh. Still, they seems nice kids.

'Yer told yer parents we're here?' I asks em, tryin to sound casual like.

They shakes their heads.

'Well,' I says, 'that case, can yer keep a secret?'

This time one of them nods.

'What's the matter,' I says, 'cat got yer tongue? Or you just practisin keepin quiet?'

'Look,' I says after a bit, 'I don't know how much Michael has told yer.'

'Who?' they says.

Oh well, there's that bleedin idea of fake fuckin names out the window.

I sighs.

'The long an the short of it is that Darren is in danger, an we're hidin here for a bit. Ain't that right, Darren?' Darren nods. 'So, it's very important that you doesn't say nothin to nobody about us. Understand?'

'Yes,' they says.

'No-one knows we've taken potatoes,' says one.

'Nor milk,' says another.

An I really feels like I can trust em. Thank the Lord, I says.

After a bit the kids, an Darren of course, goes off to play.

Come back for lunch, I says. Sounded like his bleedin mother, didn't I, issuin all these bleedin instructions. Cept I doesn't wear pink angora, an I doesn't condone wallopin him about the place neither.

Just as they're chargin down towards the river, I calls to em to stop a minute. Is there a post-box somewhere close, I asks. They says there's one up the hill along the road from the end of the track, built into the side of a barn. Thanks, I says, an they all goes chargin off again, yelpin an hollerin like wild animals. They don't know they bin born, do they, kids like that? They got such freedom. All that space, all that fresh air.

I trundles up an posts the card to Jim, hopin that no-one spots me along the open bit of the road, though there don't seem to be nobody about. Then I comes back an settles down with a nice drop or two of whisky.

I'm just tuckin into me second tumbler when I hears this cryin, an Darren comes burstin through the door. Before I can ask what the matter is he's rollin up his trouser leg an showin me a great scrape on his leg where he's fallen, blood rollin down his leg like tears, soakin into his socks.

I manages to lift him up, sits him on the drainin board an runs his leg under the tap. What makes him howl even louder. Then I dabs it dry with me sleeve.

'There,' I says, 'nearly good as new.'

But Darren's not havin none of it.

'I want me Mum,' he's screamin. 'I want me Mum.'

I looks up an sees three little faces peerin at me round the door. They takes one look at the scowl upon me face, an they scarpers. It's more than I can cope with, I can tell yer. But at the same time I knows it was the wrong bloody move. I knows they is gonna go home an tell about Darren screamin for his Mum.

After a bit, Darren calms down. I've lifted him down an sat him on me coat in front of the fire, got out a book. I tries to read him a story, but in the end he gets impatient with me bein so slow, an begins to read it to me, but then, real sudden like, he flings it across the room. Says he's bored with the same old books, wants sommat new.

I sighs deep.

'Darren,' I says gentle like, 'we has to go back. This ain't gonna work out, is it? I has to take yer home.'

He shakes his head.

'Look, luvvy,' I says, 'not five minutes ago you was shoutin for your Mum.'

'I don't want to see me Dad though, do I?' he says in a pathetic, whimpery little voice.

'Think about it,' I says an goes an stands at the back door, lookin out on to the garden.

The sky above the trees has turned a uniform grey, a flake or two of snow drifts down in front of me. Any rate, I thinks, we ain't goin nowhere tonight, so I closes the door an builds up the fire, an we spends the rest of the day cocooned up in our little house, playin draughts an fox an geese with different coloured pebbles what Darren's collected from the river, while Basher lies exhausted in front of the fire.

Next day we looks out an everywhere's white. When I opens the front door the snow's all blown up against it, buildin a thin framework of crystals around an oval of space to look through. The trees are laden with their weighty strips of white, the branches droopin, the ground covered in a smooth milky layer, part from the occasional stem of bracken pokin through, stickin out from the snow like drownin men's fingers. An it's still comin down in fine crystals from the thick gluey sky.

Before we've finished breakfast the kids from the farm are knockin. They're wrapped up in scarves an gloves, there's snow on their hats, makes em look like iced buns.

'Comin out, Darren?' they asks, lookin past me to where Darren's is sittin chompin his breakfast.

Darren's lookin at me for permission an I waves me hand at him, usherin him out. To be quite honest I'm thinkin that I could do with a bit of peace an quiet. Me energy's sapped.

He ain't got no wellies like the other kids, so I builds up the fire nice an warm in anticipation of a big dryin session to come. I still hadn't plucked up courage to do no washin, an all our clothes were pretty black by then. Waitin for a nice sunny day, I was.

I stands at the door watchin the kids bounce down the hill through the snow, collectin snowballs as they goes, their wild excited shots way off the mark. Halfway down they decides to carry Basher, cos he's so small he keeps disappearin into snow-drifts. I can just see his little brown head pokin out from one of the boy's jackets.

An when they've gone, I stands starin at the beauty of it all, an listens to the silence, a silence what's deeper than I ever heard before. It's as if God's got out a fuckin great hoover an sucked up all the sounds. An again I has the urge to paint it all. But how would yer paint the silence?

Darren comes back for lunch, clothes an trainers wet through, of course. He has to put on a jumper of mine that hangs on him like a dress, then stands warmin himself in front of the fire while I flusters about with a branch what I had hauled in to burn, but instead rigs up a clothes-horse of sorts, an drapes his things over. I uses a twig an toasts slices of bread, spreads em with peanut butter.

While we're sittin eatin lunch, Darren starts on about some ghost what his new pals have told him about. It lived down by the old ford, he said. A little bit downstream, apparently, though it was meant to frequent the cottage too.

It was the ghost of a woman who lived in the cottage. She was hidin her husband what was wanted for stealin, an was certain to be hanged. So when she saw the king's men comin, she decided to create a decoy while her husband sneaked away out of sight. She went down to the ford and pretended to be drownin. She knew the river like the back of her hand and knew that if she stood on a bank in the middle she could pretend to thrash about all she liked without comin to no danger like, whilst at the same time bein beside this whirlpool what she knew had claimed lives before. Anyhow, accordin to Darren, she shouted an screamed till the king's men hurried to the ford, saw a poor woman drownin, or so they thought, an two of em jumped off their horses and dived into the whirlpool to save her, where they promptly got into trouble themselves an drowned. Course, when they discovered her trick she was taken away by the others an hung for murder, but her ghost still haunts the place, an it's said that she still entices people into the whirlpool, cos there have bin three more drownins since, over the years.

'There's a few king's men I wouldn't mind drownin,' I laughs when Darren had finished his story, but Darren's serious.

'P'raps the ghost'll entice them away when they come for me,' he says.

It's the first time that he's mentioned bein found. It shakes me up. An I'm just musterin around tryin to think of sommat comfortin to say, when there's a knock at the door. The two of us nearly jumps out of our skin, we does. But it's only Kate, the eldest of the farm children. Phew, we laughs, in relief. But she ain't laughin.

'Sammy's let the cat out of the bag,' she says, still pantin from runnin here.

'What d'yer mean, ducky?' I says. 'Here, come in an have some toast, the fire's red hot.'

But she shakes her head.

'Sammy's gone an told Dad about you,' she persists.

'Oh dear,' is all I says.

After all, what else is there to say? We knew it was comin. Yeah, we'd known all along we was sittin on a fuckin time bomb.

'Are we gonna leave, Glory?' asks Darren.

'Where we gonna bleedin go to,' I mumbles.

That night I'm worried on two scores. One that Darren's gonna die of hypo-fuckin-thermia after gettin so cold an wet. We're short on blankets, an his clothes ain't dried out in time for him to put them back on to sleep in. I gives him me coat, which don't leave me with much, so I decides to stay up all night to keep the fire stoked. That way, too, I'd be able to listen if they came for him. That was the other score, tho I didn't have to tell yer that, did I?

I sits down close to the fire, leanin me back against one of the walls, an muses. Thinks about me life, I does. All what I've done with it, an all what I'd like to do. Thinks about Jim an little Darren there, the only people in me life what've been real friends. At least there's bleedin somebody, I thinks.

SIS

I've been talking to Gerald. See, Gloria wants me to take our Sally to meet her, and she wants to meet him, too. She says she hasn't got much and it would make her feel part of the family. Gerald says, where's the harm. But I don't know. I still feel protective about Sally even though she is nearly twenty-two. I don't think it's fair to connect her to that part of my past, that part that I've never mentioned to her before.

I know that Gloria's OK, and that she's no threat to us while she's in there, but then there's this doubt in the back of my mind, knowing that she always was a bit funny as a child. Gerald says she's stark raving bonkers, that they'll never let her out. I don't know where she'd go if they did, in any case.

GLORIA

I wakes with a start in the mornin, all guilty like. Me neck's stiff where I been leanin crooked up against the wall. An I'm cold. The fire's nearly out. Only a few powdery grey embers in the grate, the occasional reddish glow wormin its way along the skeleton of a twig.

Darren ain't nowhere to be seen. The makeshift clothes-horse has bin stripped of its clothes. I creaks up an goes an looks out the door. No sign there neither, but I know it's late, cos the light's bright already an the sunlight's dancin in little spangled lights upon the ice-crystals.

Then I notices the bread out on the drainin board, so I knows Darren's helped himself to some breakfast at any rate. I moves about, tryin to get some circulation goin through me body, then I cuts meself some bread, drinks back a cup of water. At that point I would of done anythin for a nice hot cuppa. Stead, I has a sup of whisky to warm me up, but there ain't much left in the bottle, so I has to make do.

In fact, there ain't much left of nothin, an I knows I'm gonna have to make another trip to the village. Tomorra at any rate if not today. An I'm wishin that bleedin Darren would come back an help me write a fuckin shoppin list. An I'm workin meself up into a right stew, thinkin that it's all very well him gallivantin off all the time, not shoulderin none of the fuckin responsibility, an it's about time he fuckin did, when he appears at the door, his eyes shinin with excitement.

'Hey,' I says, real sharp like, 'thought yer was gonna learn me to write.'

He blinks, puzzled by my greetin, then says, 'D'yer know, Glory, it's Christmas Eve tomorrow.'

Well, fuck me, I thinks, what am I meant to do about it? Just get on the hot-line to Father fuckin Christmas an order up half a dozen presents? An what we gonna have for Christmas dinner?

A lump of fuckin snow on a makeshift fuckin plate.

'Better get fuckin Christmas shoppin then, hadn't we,' I says.

An his face crumples. But straightaway I'm sorry, an goes an hugs his damp body.

'Here, boy,' I says, soft like, 'we'd better get yer dried out again.'

An while we're waitin for his clothes to dry out again Darren gets out his readin book, *Jim's Day Out*, an makes me read it to him. An that sets us thinkin about Jim. Wonder what he's doin today, I says.

We've got a problem. We've finished burnin all the sticks we'd gathered in before the snow, cept for the clothes-horse, an there's still a foot of snow outside. Looks like Christmas could be cold as well as hungry, I says to meself. So after we've done our readin I decides to get me boots on an have a bit of a poke about in the snow till I finds some twigs. It ain't easy an me hands are raw in no time, but I plods on, enjoyin meself in a strange sorta way, deep in thought about plans an stuff. So I doesn't notice them comin up the track till they're practically up behind me. Three fuckin police officers an a great fuckin bear of an alsatian. Mrs Eden, they says. I pulls meself upright an nods at em. We've got reason to suspect that you've abducted a boy by the name of Darren Paley.

To begin with I doesn't say nothin, just stands there, thinkin well, Glory, time's up, me gal. Out the corner of me eye I sees a flicker at the cottage door an knows Darren has seen em too.

'P'raps yer'd like to come into the house, Officer,' I says in the best Queen's English.

They follows me up to the cottage an we goes in. I could of come up with all sorts of cock an bull stories about bein there on me own an that, but I knew in the long run it wouldn't be no fuckin use pretendin, so I yells for Darren. But there ain't no reply. No sign of Basher neither. The cops says they're gonna search the house. No, Officer, I says, I'll get him. One of em insists on comin up the stairs with me. Don't trust me, do they, though I weren't goin fuckin nowhere. Darren, I calls, you gotta come out, but still he don't answer. Then we notices a window open. Course he's jumped out, ain't he. See, it ain't far to the ground even though it is upstairs, the cottage bein built into the side of the hill an all that. An he's scarpered. In one way I'm pleased, but then I knows he won't get very far, an if he did, I ain't at all sure how long he would survive, poor little blighter.

Course, two of the cops goes chargin after him, with the dog, while one stays with me. He's a young un, looks too young to be a fuckin cop with his baby face an all. He don't quite know what to say, just struts around the kitchen lookin around, with this sort of curl to his lips, like he's disgusted.

'What you turnin yer nose up at?' I says at last, 'Better than a fuckin cardboard box on Oxford Street, ain't it?'

An I sets about stokin up the fire with a few damp twigs, as if I was stayin there, an they was me fuckin visitors.

'Can't offer you no tea, Officer,' I says, 'but would yer like a glass of spring water?'

No thanks, he says, polite but cold as the snow outside.

SIS

Do you know, you're never going to believe this, but the more I speak to her the more I wonder about whether she did abduct that little boy. Of course they say she did. And she says she didn't. More like he abducted her, she says. But they say that's what happened, and they say you can't rely on her story, not someone like her. But in some ways what she says seems to add up and I'm not sure there isn't some truth there somewhere. Then again, there's the evidence. Like if she wasn't trying to abduct him and to deceive everyone, why did she go and dye his hair? And then there was the toilet attendant who said she'd heard crying inside the toilets. And why hide him away in a cottage in the middle of nowhere? See, you don't know what to believe, do you?

GLORIA

Course eventually they comes back with Darren. He's fuckin soakin. An so are both the bleedin constables. An all three are shiverin like fuckin jellies, their lips a queer sorta blue. The only one what is waggin his bleedin tail is Basher, who's enjoyin all the excitement.

'Found him in the bleedin river,' they tells their mate. 'Got himself up on a sand bank, could've been really bloody dangerous, but fortunately the river wasn't too high. Don't know what the bleedin hell he was playin at.'

I smiles to meself. I knows what he was playin at all right.

An now Darren's ballin his bleedin eyes out, he is. I goes up to put me arm round him, but they stops me. That annoys me, it does, but I doesn't say too much. I just tells Darren things'll be all right, though I ain't too convinced they will.

They allows us to gather up our possessions, while they makes sure the fire's out. I manages to drain the last few drops of whisky out the bottle under pretence of bein in the john. Steadies me nerves a bit, it does. Then I comes downstairs an they shuts up the cottage as best they can an escorts us along the track. As we're walkin we hears a great clatterin like a torrent crashin over rocks, but the noise is comin from the topmost branches of this great fuckin tree. I looks up to see a crowd of crows sittin up there amongst the bare boughs like great blobs of premature black fruit. Clackin an chatterin an really carryin on. They sounds like they could be laughin at me. Or cryin in sympathy. I doesn't know which. But I sure as hell knows what I feels like doin.

We arrives at the end of the track where their vehicles is parked an we're 'invited', if you please, to get into one of the cars. As if we has a fuckin choice. Darren an me are allowed to sit in the back, but we has a cop between us, so I still can't even give him a hug. Cos he's sobbin from time to time, with Basher on his knee, lookin up at him with his big brown eyes, as if he's tryin to understand what the hell is goin on.

There ain't a lot to tell after that. We has that long drive back to the Smoke, an the main thing I remembers is how fuckin tired I feels. I nods off, thinkin about Jim, thinkin that the only thing I could possibly want to get back for is to see him. Cos he's the only one what understands. An knows the truth. An I wonders, when they puts me in the clink, if he'll come an visit me, or whether he'll be too scared to come near the bleedin place. An I wonders if Darren'll be allowed to keep Basher, or whether it'd be best for Jim to have him for the duration.

When we gets there, Darren gets taken off for a medical, I believe, before them animals of parents of his takes him home. An I spends the night in the slammer. Next day, Christmas fuckin Eve, I gets remanded in custody, charged with abduction or some such item.

'What I wants to know, Constable,' I says to one of em in the police car on the way back from the courts, 'is who told you we was there, at the cottage? Was it that farmer?'

He looks at me as if he can scarcely be bothered to speak, as if I'm vermin. Then a smirk crosses his lips.

'Mrs Eden,' he says, 'you was like a sheep leavin a trail of shit behind you. Causin a rumpus in them public lavatories. Attractin attention in the village shop. But yes, you're right, the farmer did phone the local police.' He pauses. 'Course I'm leavin out one of the main clues. Left courtesy of you.'

'Me, Officer?' I says, curious like.

'You sent a postcard to yer friend, didn't yer? Same day as we was called to his flat by a neighbour an discovered him dead.'

Well, that news just about knocks me flat, it does. It's like someone's come along with a fuckin sledgehammer an knockin me full force in the chest. Or someone comin an snatchin all me insides out. I just feels like a shell. Like nothin. Like shit.

Didn't yer know, says the police officer. Didn't yer know. His voice keeps echoin in me ear. Course I didn't fuckin know,

I shouts, an lashes out at him. Course I didn't fuckin know, how the fuckin hell should I fuckin know. I'm fuckin wild, I am. I'm so wild I doesn't know what's happenin. Next thing I'm back at the nick an some medic is jabbin me with a fuckin great hypodermic full of some fuckin tranquilliser or other.

Later, durin interviews, they has the fuckin cheek to ask me if I sexually abused Darren. I can't believe it. What the fuck d'yer take me for, I says. Had I touched him, they said. Course I bleedin touched him, I was like a bleedin mother to him. Had I abused him in any other way, they says. What about those scabs an bruisin on his leg? But I'm speechless by then. Yer fuckin bastards, I says. Yer fuckin bastards.

SIX STORIES

ROBERT'S GARDEN

He doesn't notice her approach along the gravel path. He's squatting on his haunches in old grey jeans and a check shirt buttoned tight at the neck. He's busy pulling up onions, carefully easing out each bulb, rubbing away the damp earth with his thick, weathered thumb before twisting round to place it upon the pile behind him. There's a smile in his heart as he visualises bowls of soup and steaming winter stews swimming with succulent rings of the vegetable's flesh. He even straightens himself, stretches, admires the growing pile and appraises the rows still to harvest, before crouching down once more to continue with his task. And still he doesn't notice her.

He's shielded by the lavatera from the far end of the garden, and so, too, it's a few moments before she spots him. It's the lavatera that he planted only the previous autumn, already sturdy and abundant in its show of flowers, each one cupped perfectly like pink tissue-paper decorations at a craft fair. Next to that, clashing splendidly, are the tiny scarlet purses of the runner bean plant, beans already dripping their long green pendants amongst the mass of foliage. Further along, a marrow plant spreads its parasol leaves, almost to the point of obliterating the rows of carrots beside it. The ageing head of a sunflower hangs sullenly from its unwieldy stalk. And beside him, straggling stems of nasturtiums grope their way amongst the onions.

Tremain, the head gardener, moans that Robert's plot has no shape, so higgledy-piggledy are the rows; there's a clump of nettles in the corner, dandelions, Fat Hen.

'Once seeded, seven years weeding,' Tremain has grumbled more than once.

But to Robert, each plant has a purpose – nettles are for butter-flies, dandelions and Fat Hen for 'useful' insects – each plant with its special place, like the brushstrokes of vibrant colour in an abstract painting. He has spent all summer patiently weed-ing each unwanted tendril until now the garden is almost as he wants it. 'The garden.' A strip of land no bigger than ten by twenty yards, tucked away by the wall at the far end of the green-houses, in the corner of the five-acre garden belonging to Mrs Middleton-Briggs. His garden's small, but he's content.

At last he looks up, suddenly aware of her bulk as Mrs Middleton-Briggs stands in waxed coat and wellington boots watching him from the path beside his patch. She's looking uncomfortable, the direction of her focus fidgeting between the onions, the far wall and the sky. It's the look she bore when she came knocking on the barn door to offer him the job almost a year ago, the look she wears when she's determined to get her own way. Yes, she came to the barn where he was sleeping rough and proposed the job, offering, too, the strip of land and the use of the caravan. It came like a blessing, a sign that things would improve. For he was on the very edge of things, having walked out of the office, left his flat, and returned north, only to receive a rough welcome. He at least expected his family to be pleased to see him. But when he tried to explain it all, they wore just the same expression as Tremain when he passes Robert's garden. As if Robert was an unnecessary nuisance.

'You can't stay with us,' his father told him coldly.

Robert left, found lodgings. But he couldn't afford to stay there long. Besides, the landlady grumbled about the way he lay in bed all day, smoking, and finally threw him out when she discovered he'd burned a hole in one of her sheets. After that he slept rough here and there until he found the hay barn – it was relatively sheltered and out of the way of people – not that he cared much what happened to him. The depression that caused him to return north was ever tightening itself around him, choking him.

And then Mrs Middleton-Briggs came knocking at the barn door. Excuse me, she barked, barging inside and appraising the walls and roof as if she were passing judgement on someone's private residence, excuse me, but I'm restoring an old garden... the vicar mentioned that you were here and you might be looking for a job. There's a caravan, a plot of your own and a small wage. We're rushed off our feet, you see, and we could do with some help with the harvest. OK, he said, surprising both her and himself with the quickness of his decision.

The corner of land he was given was a fuzz of nettles, couch grass and buttercups, which matted the earth into an impossible grid of roots and stone. After he finished work in the main garden with Tremain, he returned there for a further hour or two, hacking at it with spade and pick-axe in turn, till his back and arms ached. The delicate skin of his office-groomed fingers and palms blistered and hardened. And slowly the earth yielded. It became his friend, as his frustrations poured into hard physical effort. And as he worked he whispered to the land almost constantly, imagining that it listened as he dug and sifted out the roots, until the whole area lay ready for the frost to break it up, like, he said to himself, a maiden inviting a lover. When snow came and there was little work to be done, he'd step out from his caravan and trudge along to his 'garden', to talk a while. There he could straighten his thoughts, keep things in perspective. Sometimes too, when he couldn't sleep, he went there at night, squatting in his thick workman's jacket, muttering to the earth. Above all he loved the frosty moonlit nights, when he sat watching the shapes and shadows of the darkness, sometimes muttering beneath his breath, other times in silence. For he had discovered the beauty of stillness. It no longer frightened him, and the roaring in his ears that had for so long been part of his depression grew less and less. He would squat there in the moonlight until the sparkling cold began to burn his cheeks, and his fingers and toes were almost numb, and then he would creep away back to the cosiness of his caravan, afraid of disturbing the silence...

Sometimes, after being up for the greater part of the night, he was late for work the next morning. Mrs Middleton-Briggs frowned but said nothing. Tremain would grumble, muttering that he would see to it Robert's pay was docked, though it seldom was.

The first snowdrops appeared. Aconites. Early crocus. Then daffodils, followed by the blossom of an early cherry. He worked in the gardens, digging and sewing, transplanting and hoeing, keeping himself to himself as far as he could, while in his own corner he sowed carrot seed, onion sets and first crop potatoes. And as he tended the garden, he felt his depression lift. He began to plan ahead, to unravel the complex pattern of paths that could be his future...

And now he's standing, smiling at Mrs Middleton-Briggs, a warmth inside him, partly as a result of the work but also still fresh from the anticipation of the cosiness of another winter in his caravan. He wants to tell her that he is going to build a small pond at one end of his strip, put in some marsh marigolds, some blue and yellow iris, water lilies, collect some frogspawn, have a few frogs. He opens his mouth to begin but there's something in her expression that stops him. Instead it is she who speaks.

'Tremain and I have been doing a bit of planning.' Her voice is sharp, her words more clipped than usual. 'We've decided to use your corner for another greenhouse. You can have a patch further over, by the fruit trees...'

But he's not listening. The earth's already pitching beneath his feet, his heart ramming his chest. They're taking my garden, is all he can think. Rage boils up within him and before he's aware of anything else, he's thrown aside his tools and leapt over the low border hedges of the main beds, tramping across the flowers, pulling up Tremain's prize dahlias, kicking at rosebushes, slinging pots of herbs at the greenhouse. Mrs Middleton-Briggs is shouting at him, and Tremain's there too, running after him, yelling. But Robert's running faster, weaving in and out of bowers and dwarf trees, yanking at them as he passes, disregarding the thorns of roses that tear and wedge into his palms as he tugs at them. Tremain's almost caught up with him, but Robert ducks and doubles back, leading his pursuers back to the far end of the strawberry bed. Then he slips from their sight through a gap in a hedge and skirts along the far wall to the gates. There he emerges in front of two open-mouthed customers, pausing to upset one last tub before storming away, tears streaming down his cheeks.

ANGEL

I have always been afraid to say what I mean. I stutter and stumble, trying to piece the sentences together. The way to cope, I have found, is to stick to the same ideas, keep the words linked together like parts in an electronic circuit, so the energy flows through in order to light up the bulb satisfactorily. Another way to look at it is, that I am a well-rehearsed actor. I deliver lines. Faultlessly. And this is why my physics lessons run smoothly.

Mnemonics are indispensable to my teaching method. Facts, cut like lengths of copper wire in plastic casing, can be handed out to students in order to make their own circuits. Because if they can do that, then the world will be at their fingertips. And that's what we owe to the next generation. You see, I like to consider myself a thinking man.

Black bastards rape our young girls, but Violet gave willingly. It was just part of the circuit of that particular lesson. Someone at training college had passed it on to me. And we thought it was funny. That's all. A useful reminder for all those blasted colour codes. I've been doling it out ever since. To Year Group after Year Group. Never had complaints before.

So you will understand when I tell you I am taken aback when Matthew calls me into his office. With regard to 'a matter of some concern'.

He furrows those dark bushy eyebrows and stares hard at me across the desk.

'Attention has been drawn,' he says, 'to certain irregularities. Mrs Jackson – '

'Ah.' I raise my eyes heavenward, allow a small smile of contempt. 'Mrs Jackson.'

One of those parents who simply did not know when to let go, always had to interfere with the workings of the school.

'This time,' the Head says, 'I'm afraid she might have a point, George. For instance, who is Violet?'

'Violet?' I hear myself echo. 'I haven't the f-faintest idea.'

'Ever made racist remarks in class, George?'

I blink, shake my head.

'You k-know me, Matthew. Sex, race, politics: strictly taboo.'

The Head stares at me.

'Then who is Violet?'

I can't think that I have met, or am likely to meet, a Violet.

The Head leans back in his chair with an impatient sigh.

'Sex, race and politics involved in this one, George.'

I am not what you might call a political animal. I get on with my day to day living, that's all. Just like anyone else. An ordinary bloke, I'd say.

The Head's putting on his reading glasses, looking down at some notes in front of him.

'*Black bastards rape our young girls, but Violet gave willingly.* That's what it says.'

Now I know what he's talking about. And I want to laugh.

'A mnemonic,' I say meekly.

It's then that he explodes.

'Christ, George, do you think that's an ethical way to teach?'

'S-sorry.'

'Sorry! Mrs Jackson and Gary are lodging a complaint.'

'I didn't mean…'

'Do you realise the damage you've done to the reputation of the school? We have an equal opportunities statement, you know.'

'Sorry.'

Black Black, *Bastards* Brown, *Rape* Red, *Our* Orange. My footsteps make the rhythm as I go back down the corridor. *Young* Yellow, *Girls* Green, *But* Blue. I know I have no alternative but to tender my resignation. I know now that the Governors will insist upon it. *Violet* Violet, *Gave* Grey, *Willingly* White. I'll go quietly.

I'm not one for chaos. I empty one drawer at a time, pack the contents neatly into a suitcase. Socks. Jumpers. Underpants. A man like me, living alone, doesn't have too much. And I'm not a hoarder. That would make for inefficiency. And efficiency is the code of our time. Keep the circuit working.

Even my books. I can almost tie them in two bundles. In one, text books. In the other, a few cheap thrillers that I picked up from a book fair and still haven't got round to reading. The ones that I have read have already gone to Smith & Dacre's Secondhand Books. Keep the circuit working.

I should have known when Gary asked me to repeat it. The disbelief in his eyes. At the time I put it down to a rather 'nice' family background, father being big with the local Liberals. I thought it was *bastards* he objected to. Change it to blokes, I'd suggested, perhaps that would be more polite. And smiled. The others in the class had sniggered.

I can't stay in this town now. Everyone knows. That's the sort of place it is. They all know me, and I know most of them. One of my pupils lives next door. Opposite, an ex-pupil has a couple of kids. Not that many of them will see what the fuss is all about. *We've always thought you were such a good teacher, Mr Lathley*. That's the sort of thing they say when they see me in the street. *Philip* (or Christopher, or whoever's parent I happen to be talking to) *always says your lessons were such fun*. Fun. Yes, they were. Even though I say it who shouldn't. A child entertained is a person trained. That's my motto.

Even after all the fuss in the newspapers, they support me. It was only meant in jest, wasn't it, they say. Ay, I say. I'm not one for trouble.

But the trouble was that the Jacksons had come up from London. They had friends from Nigeria, from Bombay. Whereas here, we hardly know what one looks like, if you get my drift. There's an Asian lad in Year Nine, and a Vietnamese in Year Seven. Her family's been in the town for years. Came in with the Boat People they did. They're different. They wouldn't be offended, I'm sure. They'd know it was only words.

There's a knock on the door. It's Mrs Willis. She gazes sorrowfully at the suitcases laid out on the bed.

'I'm so sorry to lose you, Mr Lathley. You've been such a quiet and helpful tenant.'

'Things must r-roll on, Mrs Willis.'

She takes a step or two towards me, leans forward confidentially.

'You didn't mean anything by it, did you, Mr Lathley?'

'Carbon film resistors, Mrs Willis. That's what I meant by it.'

She looks puzzled. Hesitates. Remembers the roll of black bin liners that she has in her hand, offers them to me and leaves, closing the door behind her.

Carbon film resistors. Numerical values in strips of colour. First colour, first digit. Second colour, second digit. Third colour is equal to the number of zeros. In ohms, of course. The strip to the right indicates tolerance. Gold means 5%, silver 10%. Simple. But to remember the numerical code of each colour. Some find that difficult. Mnemonics are fun. A child entertained is a person trained.

I'll be sorry to leave this flat. It's a nice place. Comfortable. Convenient. And I don't yet know where else I shall go. It's not as if I've a property to sell, or much stashed away to put a deposit on a cottage somewhere. Margaret made sure of that. Turfed me out and fleeced me to boot, I'd say. Looking back, I was an idiot. I should have fought. But at the time all I wanted was the minimum of animosity. I was hurt. I thought if I was kind and considerate to her she might take me back. So I said yes to everything.

My sister Jennifer might allow me to stay a while. Swindon. Can't stand the place. I like a good Northern town myself. Besides, I can't stand her kids. Too messy. I like neat ordered lives. Connecting the circuit. That was something Margaret and I could never agree upon. I wanted Jack and Alice to grow up with a sense of order in this chaotic world. Margaret said it was stifling them. Nonsense, I said. I always made sure there was fun in it. Like Mary Poppins, I was. I had games for everything. Hiding rations from the enemy when toy-tidying. Toothbrush soldiers when teeth-cleaning.

She won't even let me see them. Says I'm a bad influence. And it breaks my heart.

I've found a bed-sit. Not the same as my old flat, but it'll do for now, and at least I've my independence. Moving to Jennifer's was never really a goer. Besides, if I have to be in a city, this one suits me. And it's not too far away from Almoor. I'm not one to migrate, you see. A home-bird, you could say. Jennifer was the one with wings. You could say I just flapped a little bit and settled just outside the nest. Grew up in Almoor. Went to school there. Left for three years to go to training college, and fluttered back, as fast as my little wings would take me. Took up a post in a school not seven miles away. Jennifer said, how could you? But I like the familiar. I like to know where I am. And the people around are people I feel safe with. Never been very good with the unknown, though, as a teacher, you get used to meeting new faces. But that's in a context. A teacher knows what is expected, and mostly, other people know what a teacher expects of them. Keeps things in order, it does. Of course there are exceptions. Like Mrs Jackson. Who steps out of line, and throws everything into disarray.

I don't think I shall stay here very long. There are patches of damp in the corner, and the bathroom's communal. I'm used to having things to myself, doing as I like. I'd been living on my own in that flat for ten years. Anyway, it's just a question of time before I get another job. My references will be good. After twenty-two years they ought to be.

I need to go out for some provisions, and I'm just letting myself out of the front door when I come face to face with a coloured fellow. In his twenties, I'd say.

'I don't think anyone else is in,' I say. It's true. My room with its paper-thin walls has been like a morgue for most of the morning.

'That don't matter,' he says, grinning. 'I live here myself. David Mason.'

And he offers me his hand. I show how broad-minded I am by shaking it. But I don't tell him my name. Don't get me wrong, I'm pleasant enough. Despite what they said in the papers, I'm not prejudiced. I just don't like to give too much away until I know I can trust someone.

I buy a paper, bring it home, cook myself an omelette, and sit and go through the Sits Vac columns. There are a couple of posts in local schools I think I'll apply for.

I go for an interview. Despite the fact that I rehearse my lines, I don't seem to be able to get out straight what I want to say. And I'm not offered the job. Not that I want it. The school is situated on the edge of a large Asian community. Not what I'm used to exactly. Besides, it turns out that the Head knows it was me at the centre of the fuss at Beckside School.

'Don't you think, Mr Lathley,' he says, 'that a mnemonic like that, harmless as you think it to be, represents an outmoded ideology?'

I laugh.

'It was just a bit of f-fun,' I say.

'We don't find the matter amusing,' says one of the governors. She's Asian.

Makes me sick, the way we aren't allowed to laugh at things anymore. Shows a narrowness of outlook. Like I say, I like to think of myself as an intelligent man.

I never quite anticipated the wrench leaving Beckside. When Matthew told me that my resignation would be expected, I accepted it with – well – resignation. And I went through the motions – typing the letter, accepting the leaving present from Head Boy, final gathering in the staff room – as if I was in some kind of a bubble. But now. Now it's hit me. I'm the resistor taken out of the circuit. There I had a function. Now I'm lying on the workbench useless, and don't quite know where else I might fit in. After all, I'm not getting any younger.

There's a job in the *Times Ed* I think I might go for. I'm worried, though, that they might want someone fresh out of training college.

I'm worried about that black fellow. He's too friendly. Wants to chat in the corridor. I think he might be gay. You never know with these people do you. He says, what's up, Elvis. He calls me Elvis – I think it's some kind of a joke. At my expense, I might add. He says, what's up, Elvis, can't you find no job? I don't like to talk, but you can't help it when you're virtually pinned against the corridor wall and he's over six foot. I say I'm between posts. I don't know why he thinks that's funny.

I'm looking for somewhere else to stay. There isn't much choice when you're on unemployment benefit. I ring up about one place that sounds nice. The woman asks if I'm in work. I'm between posts, I say. She says, ah, when do you start your new position? When I say I'm not sure, she says she's not interested and the line goes dead.

I've been here three months now. No sign of a job. All the local schools seem to have heard about me. Don't want to know. One Head said, excellent as my references are, the governors regretted that they could not take the risk. Risk? What risk?

Weather's turned. My room seems damper, and it's difficult to heat. I dream of being back in my old flat at Almoor, going out to the warm classrooms of Beckside. Those were the days.

David – that is, my coloured neighbour – says I'm looking despondent these days, says I ought to get back to the rock 'n' roll. What, man, he says, can't you find a job, someone of your capabilities? Of course he doesn't know anything about what happened. If he did, I guess he wouldn't speak to me, he'd call me a racist bastard. He's actually not a bad fellow. Considering.

It's evening, and I'm sitting in front of my two-bar electric fire sorting out my cassette player that seems to have gone on the blink. Besides I'm tired of reading, and don't know what else to do with myself. I don't really have any friends, you see. Not here. Even at Almoor I didn't have anyone you could say I was really pally with. Not that I was really worried by it. I had friends at Beckside. The school was my social life – teaching, gatherings in the staff room. We'd often have a laugh and a joke in there. Holidays, I'd be off down to Jennifer's, or visiting Mother and Father. Before they died. And there was always preparation for the next term. Plus fixing things. That's a hobby of mine. People in Almoor sometimes called me Mr Fix-it. They'd bring me their broken gadgets – TVs, radios and the like – and more often than not, I'd get them up and running again. Just a question of making sure everything is properly connected and each individual part works. Helps if, like me, you know your electronics, of course.

Anyhow, I'm sitting there, *fiddling*, as Margaret used to call it (she hated me being out in my workshop) when there's a tap on the door. It's David. Can I come in, he says. Well, what else can I do but let him in, although I must say I feel a bit strange about it. So I sit him down and offer him a beer. Hey, man, he says, gazing at the spread of pieces on the table, what you doing?

'Fixing my cassette player,' I say. 'Could say it's my field. Used to teach electronics.'

'Is that so?' he says, leaning back into his chair and stroking his goatee beard, 'Not musical as well, then, Elvis?'

And he crackles with private laughter.

'What is it with this Elvis business?' I ask, irritated.

'It's the quiff, man,' he says, still giggling.

My hand automatically goes up to what used to be a thick forelock of hair. Now, a mere offering.

'You shouldn't make personal remarks,' I snap.

'Didn't mean to offend, man.' He pauses, becomes serious. 'As a matter of fact, I came round because there are one or two jobs going at my place. Thought you might be interested.'

'Your place?' I say, trying not to sound too disparaging.

'Pandemonium.'

'Never heard of it.'

'What, man, never heard of the craziest fun park in the area? You mean to tell me, the kids at your old school never talked about it?'

Somewhere in the back of my mind…

'It's one of those things that I've probably forgotten.'

'Forgotten Pandemonium, man?' He's sitting there with a fake hurt look.

'Not interested, you see. Fast rides. Everything topsy-turvy. Not really my scene.'

'But you'd like a job?'

'I'm a teacher.'

'Plenty of kids there.'

'My place is in a school.'

My companion tosses his head back and laughs.

'Man, d'you think any school round here's going to touch you with a barge pole?'

I don't know what he means. I stare at him.

'One look at the name on the application form. They've only been inviting George Lathley for interview so's they can see what he's really like.'

I'm shocked.

'Do you think I don't read the papers?' he continues, noticing my expression, 'I'd know that face anywhere after seeing it staring out of the front page at me, with that funny little Elvis quiff. '

My neck and cheeks are burning with embarrassment.

'Y-you know who I am, and you still want to talk to me?'

'Oh, us black bastards got big hearts, you know.' He stretches lazily and stands up. 'Besides, I reckon Teacher might be learning a thing or two.'

I've had enough.

'Goodnight, David,' I say, between gritted teeth.

'Remember, if you are interested in a job, I may be able to pull a few strings.'

I grimace at him, close him out. I don't want any of his blasted charity.

Resistors are used in electrical and electronic circuits as a means of controlling the current flow through the circuit, or a part of it. But where is the flow? Why do I feel disconnected? After all, I'm a resourceful man. I just have to change direction. Plug into a different circuit. Sometimes when things were going wrong I used to talk like that to Margaret. *Do shut up, George*, she'd say. The trouble is, I was born to teach. What else can I do? If that black bastard neighbour of mine is right, no-one'll take me. Not in this country. And what would I do abroad? Foreign countries are for holidays, and even then I'm always glad when I've got my feet firmly back on English soil. You know where you are then. What the rules are. In fact I haven't been out of England since I was with Margaret. Over ten years ago. She was always wanting to hop off somewhere or other. Why can't we stay at home for a change, I'd say. She'd get cross then. *You never want to do anything, George*, she'd say. In some ways, I suppose, I'm better off without her.

No sign of a job. The last three applications, I haven't heard a thing. Not a thing. You'd think they could let me know that they're not interested. Someone at the Job Club said that's what they do these days, or rather don't do. Saves resources apparently. When I told David and remarked that they never used to do things like that, he laughed. When was the last time you were looking for a job, man, he said. Twenty-two years ago, I said.

That's right. David and I are still speaking. I've tried keeping my distance, but he's so damned friendly. He even brought me round some pasta the other day, said he'd made too much. I didn't know what he might have put in it, these Caribbeans have some pretty funny cooking habits, so I've heard, but I tried it, and it *was* tasty. As good as Margaret used to make. What part of the Caribbean do you come from, I asked, when I took the dish back. He just about doubled up with laughter. From the banana plantations in Newcastle, man, he said. Sometimes I think he's crazy. You hear that about black people, don't you. Tendency to madness. But, in other ways, I think if he wasn't black he'd be an angel.

The Job Club is beneath me. But I have to go, because they wouldn't pay up if I didn't. Have to prove I'm interested in finding work, they say. Do they really think I enjoy sitting all day in this room with the wallpaper peeling off the walls and the sound of upstairs' telly blasting down through the ceiling? I am trained as a teacher, I'll have you know, I say to them, I could be out there teaching tomorrow's generation. Now that's what I call a waste of resources. That was when she told me that if I didn't lower my voice and calm down a bit she'd have to call her supervisor.

There was a girl in David's room last night. Could hear them giggling – and God knows what else. I kept my head under the covers. Then this morning I bumped into her in the corridor. I was on my way back from the bathroom, where she was just going. One of us, she was. White, I mean. And pretty. Big smile to match David's. It's the first thing I ask when he brings me round some Shepherd's Pie. That is, after his lecture about how I should look after myself, not let myself go just because I'm down on my luck. Have you known her long, I say. About a year, he says. She's been working abroad and now she's got a job in London, starting next week. Between posts, he smirks. Doesn't she want to find a job near here, I ask. There aren't many jobs of that calibre round here, is the reply. Funny, it doesn't quite go with my image of David, him cavorting with a high-flier. By the way, I say, just as he is going back to her, what's her name? Violet, he grins, and closes the door. Sometimes I think his sense of humour is particularly harsh.

I'm thinking about advertising. Perhaps a card in the local newsagent's to begin with. *Mr Fix-it will repair your unfixable electricals. Very reasonable rates.* I can't go on with nothing to do indefinitely. It gives me too much brooding time. Start getting choked up about not seeing the children. They'll be at university by now, and I don't even know where. Margaret, I've got over, but Jack and Alice... I have a right. They're my own flesh and blood, aren't they?

The postcard's been in the window for two weeks and not a squeak. I had a call on my mobile, which I think might have been a customer, but the line was bad, and they didn't try again. Geraldine (that's David's girl's real name) has gone down to London and the place is very quiet again – apart from the upstairs telly, that is. I've discovered that the old girl who lives there is stone deaf, so I can't really go up and tell her to turn it down.

I decide to re-word my advert and go out to put postcards around some more shop windows. Just as I am shutting my door, I see David and another gentleman of his *persuasion*, shall I say, manoeuvring a table out through his door. I look at them quizzically.

'Moving out, man,' says David. 'Can't stand the neighbours.' And bursts into peals of laughter.

Moving out? I'm stunned. He can't do that. Not just when I'm getting used to him. Besides, he's my friend.

'Th-thought you were here for the duration.' I try to sound light.

'What, man, in this dump? I've been waiting for my house to be built, that's all. Didn't I say? This was the cheapest place I could find. Couldn't afford a mortgage on the plot, to pay the builders *and* a penthouse apartment. Junior management don't pay that much, man.'

They've got the table out into the corridor and are turning it on its end ready to attempt the door before the stairs.

'Junior management?' I echo.

'Told you, George. Pandemonium.'

They disappear through the door. I follow, call down after them.

'Want another pair of hands?'

'Thanks, bring anything you like, the door's open.'

I go into his room. It's the first time I've been in there. Décor-wise, it's much the same as mine. Boxes are stacked in the middle. As for the furniture, I can't tell what's his and what is the landlord's. I lift a box from the top and carry it out to the van that's parked outside.

When most things are packed into the van, I go back to my room and put the kettle on. Make them tea. They drink it with milk and no sugar, just like me. David's friend, Peter, is a pleasant chap. Turns out he's a junior doctor at Central Hospital.

David checks his room for anything left behind, then we go down to the van. Peter and David climb in.

'Pop in on me some time,' I say. 'Though, of course, I probably won't be here much longer myself.'

Where the bloody hell else am I going to go, I think.

'I'll send you my new address,' David calls, winding the window of the driver's side down, as he pulls away from the kerb.

SOMETHING TO TELL TOMMY

We began with banana skins, me and my brother. Kneeling by the hearth, alert as rats, listening for the yelp of the door handle, the scrape of my Dad's boots against the iron grid outside the back door.

Behave yourselves, Mam had said, as she closed the door behind her.

And we'd watched from the window as she walked off down the street, her body bent forward, her coat flapping in the bitter wind. Then I fetched a chair and Michael climbed up, groped around on the shelf where we knew the matches were hidden, beside Senn's *Century Cookbook* (that used to be Grandma's) and the rent book. And nimble as a gazelle he was down again in no time, brandishing the box, a grin upon his face.

Somebody at school had told us banana skins made you high. We didn't know whether they were pulling our legs; I wasn't even sure what high was. Michael said it was like the time Mam and Dad went out to that meeting and we drank the cider in the pantry. They never left any booze around after that, and Mam was always careful to leave the matches, as she thought, 'hidden'.

It wasn't so much that I wanted to smoke. That was Michael's idea – said all his friends were doing it. The banana skins smelt disgusting, and the smoke stung my nostrils, made me splutter and choke, and burned at the back of my throat. No. It was the flames I liked, the pale, buttery flicker, dipping, then rising and peaking along the match, blue, green, colours that reminded me of pictures I'd seen of exotic places to which I had never been and could never hope to go.

We ended up with the kitchen full of smoke, had to open all the windows, thrash at the air with old copies of *The Herald*. The air was just about clear by the time Dad came home.

It wasn't long after that that Michael began to dig a hole in the garden. I don't know why. I think it was like the banana skins and the cider. He wanted to explore, discover something exciting. Mam said she didn't mind him digging the hole. Outside was a mess anyway. Mam and Dad argued about it. The mess, that is. Mam said the neighbours were complaining that the likes of us were letting the street down, that Dad really ought to do something. Dad got mad, ask how the hell was he supposed to find the energy, wasn't he all used up by the hours he put in at the Yard? Mam heaved a great sigh then, went over to Dad, all soppy, said she was sorry. We should count our lucky stars that he had a job, she said. Anyway, she laughed, there are some very healthy weeds out there. Good variety, too. Then Dad laughed, hugged Mam back.

So, they didn't object when my brother decided to dig the hole. Mam gave him a few strange looks, muttered something about a psychiatrist, but it kept him out of mischief. Out he went, hacking away alternately with Grandad's old garden spade and then the fork, digging deeper and deeper, while the mound of soil beside him got higher and higher. He dug it square and by the time he was finished it was at least five feet deep. I had to jump down into it.

It was kind of nice inside. You could see the layers of earth. The rich crust of chocolate brown soil at the top snaked with a mesh of thin white roots. Beneath that was biscuit-coloured stone that crumbled between our fingers and reminded us of Aunt Doreen's cakes, the dry ones that cloyed and clogged in your mouth. And the stone was stuck into stubborn clods of orange clay, which went down as deep as Michael had dug and

promised to go on forever. Once in, I couldn't get out without
Michael's help. I suppose we could have lowered a chair into
it, or even left an old wooden box in there to climb on, but
Michael was there, so we never bothered. Which was really
stupid. Because one day he went and forgot about me. Mam
and Dad were out, and we were messing about in the hole. Then
he said he had to go indoors for something. I waited a while and
he didn't come back. I tried to climb out, but the sides were too
slippery. I waited some more. But I got fed up. So I shouted.
There was no reply. I shouted again. And then it began to rain.
I watched as a puddle began to collect in the bottom, felt the
water ooze into my trainers and seep between my toes. And the
drips from my hair began to dribble down my neck, tickling my
back like so many cold fingers. A shiver of panic swept over
me. What if the hole filled up with water? Would I be drowned?
Or would I bob to the top like a cork, be able to scramble out,
only to die afterwards of pneumonia?

And then, at last, Michael appeared, cheerful as Larry, if you
please, whistling something by Meatloaf.

'Are you still here?' he said, as if he were surprised to see me.

'What d'you think?' I snapped. 'You know I can't bloody
get out. I could've drowned.'

He laughed. 'It were only a shower. Here, see what I've
got.'

He jumped down into the hole, and then we both crouched
down. No-one could see us, not even Nextdoor. Michael had
matches and fag papers that he'd taken from one of Dad's overall pockets. We tried rolling grass into the papers, then some of
the white roots, because Michael's friend Barry, the one who
told him about the banana skins, said that his older brother
smoked weed. I didn't like it, but I did like the golden flicker of
flame licking at the paper and the warmth on my icy fingers.

Quite soon after that Mam said we were to fill in the hole.
We complained like mad. It was our den, we said. Mam said
we were getting too old for dens. Besides, she said, Dad was

going to be doing the garden, now that the Yard was closing down.

So Michael filled the hole in, and Dad cleared the garden of rubbish and weeds, and had a big bonfire. I watched, fascinated, as flames roared skyward and the billowing smoke glowed orange in the streetlight.

Things were changing in our house. Dad was moody because he couldn't find another job, and Mam kept nagging at him, said he wasn't trying, but really she knew that Dad had less chance of a job at his age than going to the moon. We didn't laugh as much. Another couple of years, I told myself, and I'd be able to leave school and get a job in Safeway's... at least that would help.

I couldn't wait to leave school. I didn't like the teachers, except for Mr Agutter who was dead good-looking and cracked lots of jokes during lessons. Me and my friends scived off where we could. Michael was the same. Then it was time for Michael to leave. He and Dad went down to the dole together.

I got to quite like smoking. I'd pop behind the gym for a quickie in between lessons as well as during lunch break. Sometimes me and my friends were caught. The teachers didn't do much, confiscated the packet, each time threatened us with what would happen the next time. Then one day, for a dare, I lit up in the classroom. The bell hadn't gone for first lesson, and I was going to stub it out as soon as it rang. Only Mr Agutter arrived early, came in just as I was taking my first drag.

'I'll see you after school,' he said.

My friends thought it was funny, said I had a date with Mr Agutter, but I was scared. He looked stern, not joky at all. When he drove me home that night, I didn't even get a thrill from riding with him in his sport's car.

He followed me up the path to the house, asked to speak to my Dad. And I was banished to my bedroom. I lay with my ear pressed to the floorboards, straining to hear what was being said.

After Mr Agutter was gone, Dad called me downstairs. Started yelling. Where the bloody hell was I getting money for fags from didn't I know that the bloody things would kill me there better not be owt bloody else glue or crack or owt otherwise he'd beat me from here to kingdom bloody come.

I just stood there, right steady, and said, why do you smoke then, Dad?

First he turned white and then he turned beetroot. Standing glaring at me, grinding his nails into his palms. It was lucky that Mam arrived home then. Otherwise I think he might have killed me.

Mam went on at me for hours after that. Did I think I was helping any, getting Dad in a stew? Things were bad enough as they were. And now he'd be down the Black Horse spending the week's money again. I thought if I did die from smoking it might be a hell of a lot better than being in this dump.

The following night I went out with Michael and his friend Tommy, messing about down the tip. Tommy showed me how to soak rags in petrol and stuff them into milk bottles. Then we set light to the rags and chucked them amongst the rubbish, running like buggery, killing ourselves laughing when we heard the great whoomph of the explosion, daring to pause for a split second to turn to watch the wall of crimson yellow flame. Fantastic. Hey, you could set light to the school, Tommy laughed. Yeah, why not, I said.

'I really fancy Tommy,' I told Michael on the way home.

When we got to the gate, me and Michael could hear Mum and Dad rowing. When we went in, they didn't shut up either. Dad reeked of beer, Mam looked like she'd been crying. I went straight to bed.

Next day I didn't feel like going to school, but Dad said someone round here had to get a fucking education and escorted me through the gates in front of all my friends. I wanted the ground to swallow me up. The rest of the day wasn't much better either. We got caught behind the gym again, and Knockers (the Head) took all my fags. I was really pissed off.

I thought about getting Tommy in on it. Then again, it was something I wanted to do on my own. I found an old milk bottle and Dad's red can of petrol in the shed, and went down to the school. I'd been careful to pick my night, made sure there was nothing going on there, except for the usual cleaning. I knew what time the caretaker would arrive to let the cleaners in, so I hid, watching for him, then sneaked in behind him. I shut myself in Mr Agutter's stock cupboard (he never locks it) till the caretaker had finished off and all the cleaners were gone. And then came out and set to work.

First my books. I tore them up one by one. History first. That's Mr Agutter's subject. I made a pile on the floor. Then I took the folders that were on his desk, loaded on the Year 7 papier-mâché displays. I sprinkled petrol on, like vinegar on chips, thought, what the heck, and poured almost all the rest of it on in a great stinking stream. Then I stuffed the milk bottle with rags I found in the art room, soaking them with the last of the petrol, just like Tommy showed me. I stood by the classroom door, lit the match, threw the bottle into the middle of the room, and legged it.

I heard the great whoomph behind me, was aware of the light from the fire, but didn't stop to look. The fire sensors had gone off, and I was anxious to make myself scarce. The main entrance was locked, so I scrambled out the staff-room window, landing in the roses, and ran like hell, giggling me head off. I headed straight for the tip because I thought Tommy would be there, and I couldn't wait to tell him.

BEATING MEDIOCRITY

The boys stood spindly as new-born foals in their white leotards and close-fitting blue shorts, all leg. Ivory-skinned. Shoulder blades proud. They chatted to each other excitedly, waving their long thin arms, shifting their weight from one foot to another as they talked. The hum of their voices worked louder and louder until one boy caught the reprimanding eye of one of the mothers seated on the row of chairs that lined the opposite wall. He nudged his neighbour, who, in turn nudged the next boy, dominoes-style, until they all were hushed. Then the whispers again began to spiral.

Lloyd was nervous, his arms criss-crossing his stomach, clutching either side of his waist. He glanced back at his mother, who stared fondly at him, passing remarks to her neighbour, her eyes glistening with pride.

'Bless him, he's good enough,' she was saying, 'but he is highly-strung.'

On the train journey there, Lloyd had rushed off to the toilet to vomit. He had returned to his seat after a while, saying that he didn't want to go through with it. She had treated him indulgently, discarding his words like the wrapper round a sweet packet, knowing that inside true talent lay.

She nodded to him encouragingly, but he turned from her, joined the growing hubbub, until the arrival of a tall matronly woman cast instant quiet.

Madame stood gracefully poised, her grey hair drawn neatly

back into a severe bun, pinned just above the nape. A crisp white collar emerged – just so – from a smart bottle-green suit. Hands clasped together, she waited for absolute silence, then gave an unnecessary cough.

'I am pleased to announce the names of those boys required to remain for the second stage of the audition.' And began to read from a list passed to her by an assistant.

Lloyd's mother let out a small huff of relief when she heard her son's name. Disappointment at this stage would have been unbearable. After all her effort. All those Saturday journeys to this ballet school on top of those lessons during the week at the local class.

It had been the local teacher who had first spotted Lloyd's talent. Worth nurturing, Mrs Plater, she'd said. It was something Lloyd's mother had expected. She had been picked out herself, encouraged. She had danced her way all up the grades and would have gone on… but that was water under the bridge, she used to tell people, it was no good resenting things. Anyway, she would make sure there were no obstacles for Lloyd, and she would gain almost as much pleasure from his success as she would have done from her own.

With a gracious smile, Madame returned the list to the assistant and led the selected boys back towards the audition hall, whilst those disappointed dressed slowly and left.

Lloyd's mother tried to edge complacency from her thoughts. After all, she told herself, there was still this second stage, the final weeding out. In half an hour she and Lloyd might be leaving glum-faced. Not that it would necessarily be the end of his dancing career – there *were* other avenues – it was just that this was the best. And most of all she didn't want him to settle for the mediocre. Living, like her, in an ordinary little house just like all the other ordinary little people in that ordinary little street. She wasn't exactly unhappy: her husband was good to her; they didn't struggle for money like some families she knew. But somehow she thought life could be better, more *special*…

The boys returned from the hall. They looked tired now, their shoulders limp, their foreheads moist. Lloyd offered his mother a small tight smile, began to tug at a shirt mixed amongst the pile of clothes beside her.

'Well?' she asked eagerly.

He shrugged, beginning to dress. Then, Madame appeared once more. She clapped her hands twice for attention and began to speak. The competition had been extremely fierce, she said, the standard high. It was regrettable that the School wasn't in a position to offer more than three places at present. She hoped that those who were not selected this time might try again next year. Get on with it, Lloyd's mother thought, *get on with it.* Could the parents of the successful boys please collect a registration form and a list of uniform requirements before departure. A formal offer of a place and further information would be sent in the post to each of the boys in the next few days. *Get on with it.*

Lloyd Plater.

The name rang across the room. Other mothers were turning to shake her hand, as if she were in a dream. She heard herself offering congratulations to the other two chosen, commiseration to the others. She felt sorry. It was a pity that there weren't more places. But Lloyd had got through! She hugged him, though she knew he wasn't keen on hugs in public places. And it was to this that she attributed his uneasy smile.

He was subdued on the journey home, picked at the packed tea she had brought though she had been careful to include his favourite things. She put it down to tiredness, but worried the next day when he remained unusually quiet. Perhaps he's sickening for something, she thought.

Two days later the envelope arrived through the post. Lloyd had gone to school – he seemed well enough – and his mother eagerly anticipated his arrival home so that they could open the envelope together, to know for certain that this wasn't just a wonderful dream.

It was when he arrived home and sat at the kitchen table with his hot chocolate and a biscuit in front of him, the envelope un-opened beside him, that she at last had her first inkling.

'Aren't you going to open it?' she asked nervously.

With a sigh he picked the envelope up, tore at the top, removed the contents, glanced at them and lay them unenthusi-astically back upon the table.

'What's the matter, Lloyd?'

'I'm not going, Mum,' he said. 'I'm going to stay at the comp.'

She gave a false little chuckle.

'Lloydy! I know it's a big step, but you'll be fine. I promise. *Fine.*'

'I don't want to go, Mum. I don't want to dance. Not forever.'

The words slapped at her, creating a cold numbness inside.

'If it's not what the lad wants…'

She hadn't seen her husband in the doorway behind her, nor been aware that he'd come in in time to hear.

'I want to play football, Dad. They don't play it at Ballet School.'

'There'll be other things,' his mother cried. 'Dancing will be your career.'

'I don't want to dance, Mum. It's you that wants me to dance.'

Lloyd's mother turned to her husband, appealing to him with her eyes.

'But after all this work, the expense… he's so much talent. He can't waste it…'

'He'll be good at other things,' her husband said.

'But it's what I've wanted for him ever since he was born…'

But even as she said it, she knew that she was beaten. She turned away, biting viciously on her bottom lip as she chopped onions and carrots for the evening meal, great sobs churning in the pit of her stomach.

THE GIRL

At first it was said in the village that the two women were sisters. Then, on discovering their names (Connie Bell and Antonia Alberto – the latter of Italian extraction), it was rumoured that they were friends whose lovers had both been killed in the war. But as time wore on, word spread, corroborated by Johnson the plumber, who had work to carry out in their cottage, that in fact no such loss had occurred, that the two women were a couple.

Because of this, the villagers half-expected, half-wanted, the incomers to keep themselves to themselves. But Connie and Antonia did not. Both went to church. Antonia signed up for the flower rota and for weekly whist in the village hall, while Connie became secretary of the tennis club and eventually got herself elected to the parish council. All this, in addition to going out to work, Connie as a teacher, and Antonia nursing away at one of the city hospitals. Unselfconsciously, they had 'come out' before the phrase even existed.

In time, the villagers came to tolerate the 'unusual' arrangement, forgave the two women for what some of them muttered was a sin, because Miss Bell and Miss Alberto seemed 'such grand lasses'. They forgave them, just as they had forgiven Daisy May from the back lane who had, at the end of the war, somewhat shamelessly allowed herself to be seduced by an American GI (several, some said) only to produce, unmarried, a 'bonnie bairn' precisely nine months later. Indeed, scowling and clucking had turned to rummaging and clicking as everyone in the village scoured their cupboards for old woollens which they could unravel in order to provide enough wool (knitting wool itself being so scarce) to knit an entire layette for the wayward girl in time for the happy event.

Thus, when Antonia passed away in her sixty-fifth year, it was with no hesitation that the village people flocked to Connie's side, providing endless flowers and wreaths, buns and homemade wine for the tea, and many kind words to mop up Connie's tears. It did not diminish her grief, but all the same Connie was comforted to think that she had so many friends.

Then, the following year, something happened to Connie Bell that made her wonder if she had been right to think of them in this way.

Early one morning, Connie slipped into her old mac and wellies, and set out over the fields towards the river with Matt, her terrier, for his first walk of the day. She sauntered along, enjoying the mildness of the autumn weather, a light breeze upon her face, the peppery scent of oak leaves rotting in the grass. At the river's edge she stood for a while as Matt sniffed here and there, watching the water's lazy flow, admiring the rich vermilion of the hawthorn berries that edged the river bank, listening to the tractor already hard at work, grinding its way up and down the field.

She was about to retrace her steps, when she noticed Matt in the undergrowth, snuffling and wagging his tail, then whining in a worried kind of a way. Connie peered closer and was surprised to see a girl, perhaps fifteen or sixteen years old, lying asleep in the grass. The girl's skin was unusually pale and for a moment Connie's heart thumped as she thought that the girl might in fact be a corpse. She bent forward, leaning over her, and was about to touch the girl's cheek to see if it was warm when the girl opened her eyes and jerked away.

'Are you all right?' Connie asked.

'Miss Bell,' the girl grunted as she realised it was Connie. She stretched back her head, rubbing the nape of her neck with her hand.

Connie tried to remember the girl's face. There were so many young people in the village these days, and they grew up so quickly.

'It's…?'

'Lisa Tuppard.' The girl gave the information begrudgingly.

Tuppard. Yes, Connie knew the girl's mother. They lived on the estate at the far end of the village.

'Have you been here all night?' Connie asked.

The girl looked away, trying to conceal tears.

'Why don't you come back to the cottage?' Connie coaxed. 'You can warm up and have some breakfast, then I'll take you home.'

'I don't want to go home,' said the girl.

'I don't want to pry,' said Connie. The girl sat opposite her, wrapped in Connie's dressing gown, freshly bathed, her hair hanging straggly in rats' tails, colour slowly seeping back into her cheeks as she nibbled at buttered toast and sipped tea. 'But if there's any way I can help…'

'Folks always say how kind you are,' the girl said without smiling, 'but I don't think there's owt you can do.'

'I could try,' said Connie.

'I'm up the duff,' the girl announced brusquely.

'That's not such a sin these days, is it?' said Connie.

The girl leaned forward, met Connie's eyes. 'By the way Mam's goin' on, you'd think I'd murdered somebody. She says I've ruined me life.'

'Not ruined,' said Connie.

She felt awkward. It was ten years since she'd retired from teaching. Somehow she'd fallen out of the habit of dealing with teenagers. The two lapsed into silence.

'Miss Alberto were kind too, weren't she,' said the girl at last. 'She were good to me grandfather before he died. *No need to nurse me*, he'd say to her, *when you've done a day's work in that hospital*, but she'd always call round, checked that he had all he needed.'

Connie's eyes moistened.

'We're both alone now, aren't we?' said the girl. 'You, because you've lost someone; me, because there's someone growing inside.'

Connie felt sorry for her. At the same age, she had not fitted in with her parents' expectations either. It was too young an age to be cast aside, put on the scrap heap.

'I'll telephone your mother to let her know where you are,' she said. 'She'll be worrying.'

'She won't,' said the girl.

And the girl was right. The mother's reply was sharp.

'I dint care where she is. I chucked her out last neet. She can go where the bleedin heck she likes,' and the line cut off.

The next day, at the post office, Connie was surprised by the frosty greeting she received from Mrs Thripp, the postmistress. The woman scarcely managed a syllable of greeting when usually it was hard to stop her talking.

Blow me, she said to herself, word's got around that I'm harbouring the 'wrong-doer'.

Days passed and the villagers remained distant. Connie was unperturbed.

'They'll come round,' she told the girl, convinced that, as with Daisy May all those years before, they would soon begin to accept the situation and make the best of things.

Connie enjoyed the young girl's presence in the house. And in the safe environment of Connie's home, the girl became relaxed and cheerful. She chopped kindling, vacuumed around the house, carried in buckets of coal, jobs that Connie had begun to find difficult now there was arthritis in her hip. And so the girl stayed on.

In the evenings she waited at tables at a local restaurant, paid most of her wages to Connie to help towards the bills. And Connie encouraged the girl to study, helped her work towards exams for the following summer.

'You can stay as long as you like,' Connie said one evening, just as the girl was preparing to go out to work. 'We could convert the spare room into a nursery. There's room for a cot as well as your bed. And I could look after the child some of the time, while you study.'

The girl gazed at Connie with her intelligent eyes.

'The village won't like it, you know.'

'They'll get used to it,' Connie replied. 'There are single mums all over the place.'

The girl blushed, looked uncomfortable.

'It's not just that…' she began, but was interrupted by a knock at the door.

It was Ron Fowler from the parish council.

'Parish business, Ron?' Connie said cheerfully, beckoning him in.

'You could say that,' said Ron without looking at her, pretending to run his eye around the room, one that he had been in many times before.

'I'd best be going,' said the girl.

'No.' His tone was sharp. 'If you don't mind hangin' on a minute, I'd rather you heard. I shan't take long.'

Ron refused a seat, stood on the hearth, his head slightly bowed, his hands down in front of him, nervously passing his car keys from one fist to the other.

'The parish council have decided,' he began, regurgitating the words of a well-practised speech, 'that due to the particular circumstances that you have entered,' his head bobbing meaningfully towards the girl, 'that it would be better if you were to resign your position as councillor.'

'I don't understand,' Connie blinked. 'I've been a councillor in this parish to most people's satisfaction, I hope, for thirty-five years.'

'That's as maybe,' Ron said, with a snide expression, 'but folks are talkin'.'

And he bobbed his head for a second time towards the girl, who had sat down, hands folded across the small round of her belly.

'And what are they saying?' asked Connie irritably. 'Can't you give the girl a chance?'

Ron gave a small embarrassed cough.

'It's not Lisa… There's talk that she's goin' to stay here with the bairn.'

'And so she is.'

'It's not right, Connie. A woman of your... persuasion... putting wrong ideas into the lass's head, and the bairn when it arrives.'

Connie could scarcely believe what she heard. The implication, if she'd understood right, that she was having a thing with this girl, a girl young enough to be her grand-daughter, was so ludicrous that she almost laughed out loud. And would have done, had it not been for the fact that she realised that she was being pressurised to give up the opportunity to provide this girl and her child with their only real chance in life.

'I'll want a decision by the end of the week,' the man was saying. 'If Lisa decides to go, of course, we'll reconsider our request.'

And Ron left, clicking the front door behind him. Connie turned to the girl.

'I never dreamt...' she cried. 'You never thought...?'

The girl shook her head.

'Of course not.'

The next day the girl came down to breakfast, a small plastic bag in her hand.

'Not much luggage,' she smiled dolefully.

'You don't have to go,' said Connie.

'I do. The village is too small. And they'd make your life a misery. I'll go to Bradford. I've a friend...'

'I'll take you to the station,' Connie said. 'But you're always welcome here...'

When she returned, the house felt cold and grim, as it had during those first weeks after Antonia's death. There was an uncomfortable silence, broken only by the occasional swish of a passing car along the wet road outside, a solitary fly buzzing in the window. Connie went into the study and began to compose a letter of resignation.

T'AIN'T LONG TILL SATURDAY

'T'ain't long till Saturday.'

That's what he said as he went out the door. I was going to say, hang on a minute, but we've only just had Saturday, it's only Sunday night, that's six more days till the next one. But he was gone. Couldn't get out quick enough. I could already hear his car revving up in the driveway. I knew he was sick and tired of me moaning. Not that I meant to moan, it's just the way things come out these days. See, I've no-one to talk to most of the time, and I've got all these things whizzing round inside my head. When my son, Brian, turns up, or daughter Ursula and the bairns (thankfully, usually not with that great lump of a husband of hers), I am pleased to see them. And I do try not to start on about things.

I'm dead quiet to begin with, ask them a bit about themselves and that. They ask me how I am, and I say *fine*, and then they say, and have you got any news, Nan (they call me Nan in front of the bairns). As if *I* would have any news. What do they want me to say? I saw a bird land on the lawn this morning; yesterday the butcher's van called? Because that's about the sum of my news. Or did they want to know that I decided to wash my tights out by hand because I thought there wasn't a big enough wash to go in the machine?

No.

So when they come, I try to be quiet. But it's like opening a bag of sugar to fill up the sugar bowl: you make a little snip with the scissors but you only get a silly little trickle of crystals, so you pull at the corners just a little bit more and then the whole lot comes out in a great whoosh, drowning the sugar bowl and spilling all over the table cloth.

Ursula's lips tighten when I start. The eyes glaze over. And I think to myself, what am I saying it all for? Because it's clear she's not listening. And yet I keep going, just like the sugar. It's not any different with Brian. His eyes wander around the room, then he gets up and asks if it's OK to check the football scores on TV.

I talk mostly about Sam. The good times we had together. What we might have been doing this week if he was alive. What we were doing this time last year. Sometimes I go further back. To teen years. To happy times. I don't dwell on the downs. I just like to live the good bits over again. Because I'm not really living now. Not really living.

And then I get on about that to them. How I don't want to be here. Not without Sam. You see, Sam and I did everything together. When I went out, it was with Sam. When we had friends round, it was because Sam asked them.

Course, before he retired he'd be out at work in the day, and I did my little job in the bakery. But I used to live for the week-ends. Just like now, but different. Because then it was so's Sam and I could be together, and now, it's so's I can have a moan at someone that doesn't want to listen.

When Sam retired, he sold the van and all but the tools he would need for about the house and the odd little job on the side, and I packed in my job straight away. How thankful I am for that. Otherwise I'd be sitting here regretting that we didn't spend more time together when we had the chance.

Ursula says I should take up a hobby. Something to get me out of the house, take my mind off things. But what would I do? She brought me a list of evening classes for the new term, but there wasn't much on it. Ursula suggested Spanish for beginners: well, what would I be doing learning Spanish at my age when I've small chance of going to Blackpool, let alone Spain? Besides, I'd be no good at it. Sam always said I wasn't one for languages. He had a smattering of French, so he said (though I don't think I ever heard him use it), but Sam said I was better sticking to my own language. Then there's furniture upholstery... why don't you have a go at that, Nan, says our Ursula, you're still fit, aren't you? Well, fit I might be, I says, but Sam always said it was better if he did the handiwork in our house, and I kept to the stew and dumplings (and I can cook a nice stew and dumplings). Besides, when Sam passed on, I gave the rest of his tools to Brian.

Then what about calligraphy, says our Ursula, you've always taken a pride in your handwriting. I says, yes, it's all very well, but how am I going to get there on those dark and rainy evenings. I won't be wanting to go out then, not on my own. Ursula gets cross then, grabs hold of a bairn by each hand, just about drags them down from the table, where they are busy enjoying one of the little cakes I had baked for them, and went charging off home without scarcely a goodbye. She apologised next time she came, of course, said something about being worried about me. I said, don't you worry about me, I'll be all right. Then she brought out a day-classes timetable. No calligraphy, she said, but what about sugarcraft, you know how you like things like that. Ursula, I says, Ursula, how would I get there? You and Brian are both out at work, and there's no bus at all that runs that way. Besides, I'm not too keen on going to new places on my own.

Course, I says to her, Sam would have taken me, if... Get real, she says. You can tell she's cross, cos she calls me Mum and not Nan. She says, 'Get real, Mum, d'you think Dad would have approved of you going to a sugarcraft class or any class for that matter? You can be sure he would have booked up a game of golf so's not to take you.'

Well, we nearly fell out seriously then. How dare you, I says, how dare you cast a slight upon your father? After all he did for you. Worked all those years to bring you up, and you begrudge him a game of golf?

You really don't see, do you, Ursula says. But I think I see very well. I know what an ungrateful little vixen she can be.

It's not that I mind Brian or Ursula not visiting during the week. I know their lives are busy what with work and the children and that. I know that the only one who might spare the time to call is Pam, Brian's wife, and frankly, I'd rather she didn't. We don't get on. I think that they both know I don't appreciate her visits – that's why she hardly comes. Pam's too pushy, you see, likes to poke her nose in where it's not wanted. Once, she even had the nerve to arrange a place for me at a day centre. What do I want with going to a place like that, full of old fogies rabbiting on all the time. It would drive me mad. Besides, Sam would never have approved of me going out like that, mixing with other men. That's one thing for certain. I'll always be faithful to my Sam and his memory. No meeting up and getting married, age seventy-five, to some widower or other that I've met at a tea dance. Oh no.

Ursula says why don't I mix in the village. Well, Sam and I have always been independent. No going round to neighbours for cups of sugar. We always felt that there was nothing that the family couldn't help out with. Familiarity breeds contempt, as Sam used to say. So I never bothered much when people called, after the funeral and such. Was I all right, they'd ask. Yes thanks, I'd say, *fine*.

Sometimes I see Brian go past in his work van during the day. Why couldn't he just pop in for a quick cup of tea, I think to myself, it would hardly put him out at all, and it would be so nice to see him. I said to him the other day, why don't you come and eat your lunch at our house, instead of having to sit in that van in the pouring rain – you could have a fresh cup of tea, not that stale old stuff in your flask. But he's never taken me up on it. Such a shame – it would break up the week, make it seem not such a terrible long wait until Saturday.